1

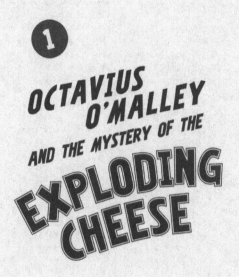

OCTAVIUS
O'MALLEY
AND THE MYSTERY OF THE
EXPLODING
CHEESE

OCTAVIUS O'MALLEY
AND THE MYSTERY OF THE
EXPLODING CHEESE

ALAN SUNDERLAND

Angus&Robertson
An imprint of HarperCollins*Children'sBooks*

Angus&Robertson
An imprint of HarperCollins*Children'sBooks*

First published in Australia in 2006
by HarperCollins*Publishers* Australia Pty Limited
ABN 36 009 913 517
harpercollins.com.au

HarperCollins*Publishers*
Level 13, 201 Elizabeth Street, Sydney NSW 2000, Australia
Unit D1, 63 Apollo Drive, Rosedale, Auckland 0632, New Zealand
A 53, Sector 57, Noida, UP, India
1 London Bridge Street, London SE1 9GF, United Kingdom
2 Bloor Street East, 20th floor, Toronto, Ontario M4W 1A8, Canada
195 Broadway, New York NY 10007, USA

National Library of Australia Cataloguing-in-Publication data:

Sunderland, Alan, 1959– .
   Octavius O'Malley and the mystery of the exploding cheese.
   1st ed.
   For primary school aged children.
   ISBN 978 0 20720 048 9.
   ISBN 0 207 20048 3.
   I. Redlich, Ben. II. Title. (Series: Octavius O'Malley
   series; bk. 1).
A823.2

Cover and internal design by Darren Holt, HarperCollins Design Studio
Cover illustration by Ben Redlich
Typeset in 11.5 on 17pt Weiss by HarperCollins Design Studio
Printed and bound in Australia by McPhersons Printing Group
The papers used by HarperCollins in the manufacture of this book
are a natural, recyclable product made from wood grown in sustainable
plantation forests. The fibre source and manufacturing processes meet
recognised international environmental standards, and carry certification.

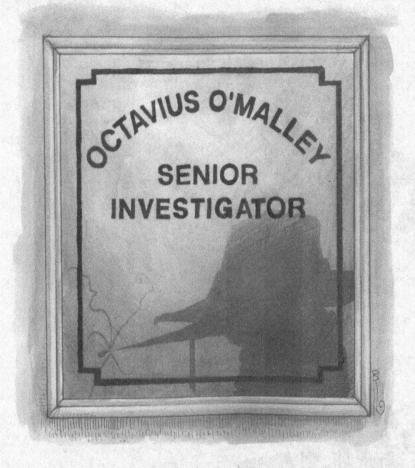

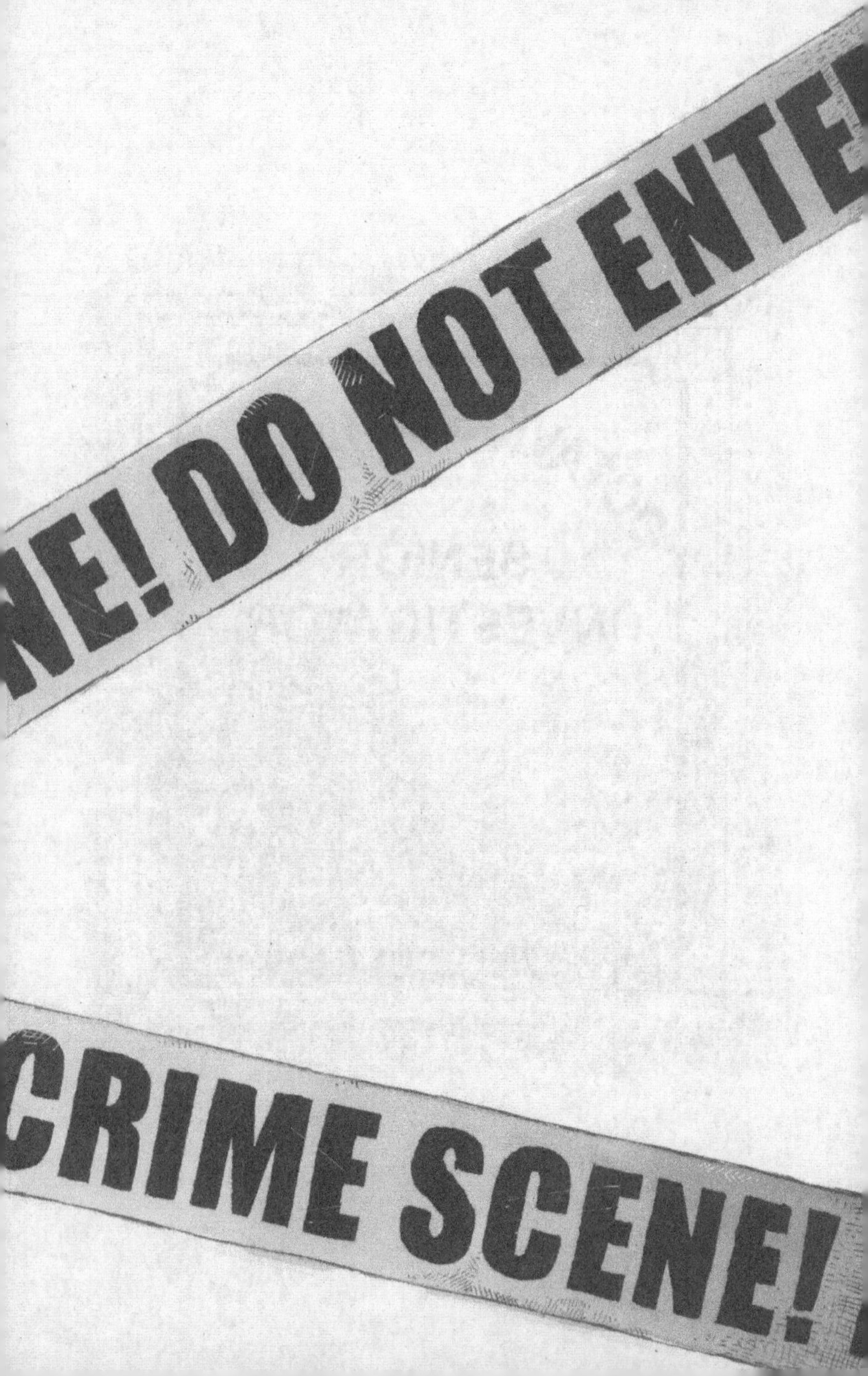
NE! DO NOT ENTE
CRIME SCENE!

1
CHEESE

The room was a mess. It looked like a bomb had gone off in there.

Not surprising, really, because a bomb **had** gone off in there. And when a bomb goes off inside a cheese factory storeroom, believe me, it's not a pretty sight.

The furniture had been smashed to bits; there were splinters of wood, lumps of plaster and pieces of twisted metal scattered everywhere. One wall was impaled with a table leg and bits of broken chair were strewn in all corners of the room, not to mention broken glass, exploded tins, shards of crockery and burnt scraps of paper.

But all of that was nothing compared with the cheese.

Great steaming globs of it stuck to the walls, huge strings of it dangled like stalactites from the ceiling, smelly yellow piles of it covered most of the floor. Sticky, runny, disgusting cheese covered every available surface, blackened here and there by the bomb blast. It was as if a cheese volcano had erupted in the centre of the storeroom, spraying out a molten mess of cheddar, camembert and stinky blue-vein lava.

As I picked my way delicately through the gunk, I wondered idly whether I'd ever seen a worse crime scene in ten years of investigations.

As my foot slipped on a piece of soft gruyère, I decided I hadn't.

There's a reason why I know so much about crime scenes. I am a detective, and a good one too. Ten years on the police force, rising from a humble constable to a senior investigator. Inspector Octavius O'Malley is the name, although most of my friends, a few of my enemies, and all of the junior officers who work for me call me Ocko.

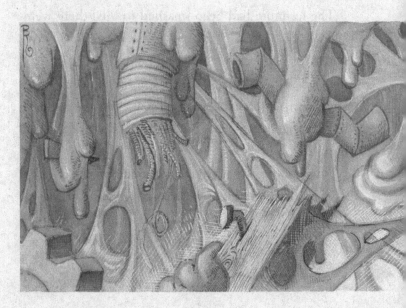

Which was what one of them did right now as I picked my way cautiously through the cheese-spattered debris.

'Hey, Ocko, have a look at this!'

Sergeant Smith waved me over to the doorway, where he was crouched down examining a particularly large mound of melted cheddar. As I headed in his direction, my arm brushed against the wall and a greasy smear of cheese stuck to my fur. I brushed it away.

Fur? I can already see you looking up from this book with a puzzled expression on your face. **Fur? On his arm?**

Well, of course I have fur on my arm. On both my arms, in fact. And my legs and my face and all over my

body. You don't have to look so surprised; it's perfectly natural for a **rat**.

I tell you I'm a rat, and right away you don't like me. Don't bother to deny it; I know it's true. **Yuck** you cry! **A rat! Rats are dirty, smelly, sneaky little pests. They carry disease, they live in rubbish dumps, they stink!** Well, pardon me for living.

I've heard all the insults. **You're a dirty rat**, they say. **Don't rat on your friends**, they say. **He's like a rat deserting a sinking ship**, they say. But how much do you humans — you monkey people — really know or care about us rats?

You call us dirty, but we spend most of our time cleaning up your mess. It's not us who leave mounds of rubbish everywhere; we just engage in a little creative recycling. You call us sneaky and cowardly, but I prefer to think of it as being smart and sensible. If a ship were sinking, why would anyone want to hang around? And if we happen to work that out before you monkey people, what does that say about **you?**

And don't even get me started on whose fault the Plague was! I know my history, believe me, and the rats were framed. Before the Plague came along, rats ruled. But after that fit-up and all the bad press we got, things went rapidly downhill.

Anyway, let's not get into a slanging match here. I'm a rat, and I'm proud of it. Rats are fine upstanding members of society, and I'd trust a good rat over a monkey person any day of the week. Mice, on the other hand, are a totally different proposition. Small, sneaky, and dumb as cardboard boxes. Don't get me started on mice.

So if you want to hear my story, you're going to have to get over any prejudice you might have about rats. And believe me, you **do** want to hear my story. It's a sensational story. In fact, we'd better get back to it, because we're still standing in the middle of an exploded cheese factory, and Sergeant Smith is trying to get my attention ...

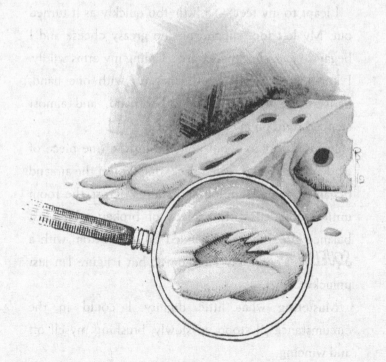

'Hey, Ocko, have a look at this!'

I joined Sergeant Smith in the doorway and crouched down to see what he was pointing at.

'See?' he said, showing me a spot on the side of the slab of melted cheese.

There, caught in the cheese and perfectly preserved, was a tiny, four-toed footprint.

As I examined the small but perfectly formed clue, I could hardly contain my excitement.

At last! After years spent chasing the most notorious crime gang in the city, it looked as though I finally had the one thing that had always eluded me: **a clue**.

I leapt to my feet — a little too quickly as it turned out. My left foot slipped on the greasy cheese and I began to cartwheel backwards, flailing my arms wildly. I knocked Sergeant Smith's hat off with one hand, banged the wall with the other hand, and almost stepped right on my beloved clue.

In my effort to avoid obliterating the one piece of evidence we had, I reeled back, one foot in the air, and began hopping, slipping and sliding across the room until I collided with a piece of broken table, lost balance altogether, and landed on my bottom with a *SQUELCH*. People say I'm clumsy, but I figure I'm just unlucky.

Mustering what little dignity I could in the circumstances, I stood up slowly, brushing myself off and wincing.

'Scrape it and bag it, Smith,' I said, pointing to the cheesy footprint. 'Get it down to the lab as fast as you can. This could be the break we've been looking for.'

Smith did as he was asked, although for some reason he looked as if he were trying to suppress a fit of giggles. I can't imagine why.

It was all starting to come together nicely. An explosion in a cheese factory. Devastation and destruction. And now, a footprint that could only have come from a mouse.

In my book, that could only mean one thing.

THE RIVER ROAD MOUSE GANG.

2
THE RIVER ROAD MOUSE GANG

I sat in my office down at police headquarters with a very large file on the desk in front of me.

Written on the front of the heavy brown folder were the words **RIVER ROAD MOUSE GANG**.

Inside the folder were dozens of incident reports, profiles, records of interview and newspaper articles.

For the past two years, I'd been tracking this notorious gang of mice as they ran riot through the city. Disrupting public events, holding up banks, terrorising innocent rats.

And in all that time, not one of these mice had been identified.

I opened the file and skimmed over a couple of newspaper stories.

For a brilliant police officer like me, it made for depressing reading.

MOUSE GANG STRIKES

A gang of vicious mice calling themselves the 'River Road Mouse Gang' held up the First Rodent Bank yesterday, escaping with more than $25,000 in cash and gold bars.

Five masked mice carrying guns entered the bank just before noon. They handed over a note claiming that they were the River Road Mouse Gang, and demanding money as payment for the 'evil persecution of innocent mice by rats of all nations'.

The guns were left behind as the gang fled, and were later found to be water pistols.

EVIL MOUSE GANG HOLDS CITY TO RAN$OM

Rodent City was without electricity for almost four hours yesterday, as the notorious River Road Mouse Gang held its most daring raid ever.

The mouse gang took control of the main power station and cut supplies to the city, leaving only an emergency backup supply for hospitals and doctor's surgeries.

The gang only restored power after city authorities agreed to their demand to display a large neon sign on the main road reading WE LOVE MICE.

Police say they are baffled as to the identity of the gang members.

RIVER ROAD GANG STRIKES AGAIN

The River Road Mouse Gang, responsible for last month's bank hold-up, has struck again.

Police say five masked mice were seen entering the Main Road Bakery just after midnight.

Staff at the bakery were locked in a storeroom and the gang immediately halted all production of bread.

They fled just before dawn, and drivers arriving for the morning bread run instead found hundreds of trays of currant buns with the words **FREEDOM FOR ALL MICE** in pink icing on the top.

The bakery vault had also been emptied of more than $10,000 in cash.

A series of daring raids and crimes, and no real clues. The River Road Mouse Gang had made fools of the police for far too long. **But not any more!**

Finally they'd made a mistake. Something must have gone very wrong at that cheese factory, something that made the gang flee before they could carry out whatever devious plan they had in mind. And now, in their haste, they had left behind a clue. A clue that could break this whole case wide open.

I shut the folder, pushed it to one side, and put my feet up on the desk. Leaning back with my hands behind my head, I started to imagine my triumph …

'Ladies and gentlerats, thank you for coming along to this press conference at such short notice. I am Detective Inspector Octavius O'Malley of the Rodent City Police, and I am here to tell you that the River Road Mouse Gang has been captured at last.'

(Gasps all around as the assembled reporters realise what a stunningly brilliant and clever detective I am, followed by spontaneous applause and wild cheering.)

'Now, now! Quiet, please. There'll be plenty of opportunity for all that later. What I'd like to do now is take you through the investigation from start to finish, so you can understand the high level of police work, thorough attention to detail and sheer brain power that was required to catch these evil villains.'

(At this point, the Mayor and the Police Chief rise to their feet, and call for three cheers for the magnificent Ocko.)

**'HIP HIP HOORAY!
HIP HIP HOORAY! HIP HIP …'**

There was a loud knock on my office door, scaring the fur off me (not really) and waking me from my daydream. I was so startled I fell backwards off my chair, sending the folder to the floor.

'Come in!' I yelled, as I began to gather the scattered papers together and stuff them back into the folder.

I looked up and saw Sergeant Smith in the doorway. He sighed, rolled his eyes and shook his head.

'Just tidying up, Smith,' I said breezily. 'How can I help you? Surely the results from that footprint aren't back from the lab yet?'

'No, sir,' said Smith, stepping up to my desk. 'But this note came for you a moment ago.'

He held out a small white envelope.

I tore it open, unfolded the piece of paper inside and read it. It didn't take long to read.

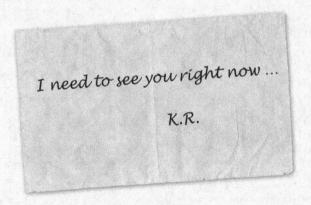

I need to see you right now ...

K.R.

This was an important note, from an important rat.

There weren't many rats in the city who could send me such a rude, demanding note and be sure that I would immediately obey.

But Kurt Remarque was no ordinary rat. A former Mayor, a leading businessrat and the biggest property owner in Rodent City, Kurt Remarque was accustomed to being listened to. He had enough money to buy the whole city three times over, and the only reason he hadn't was because he loved his money too much. And the only reason he wasn't still the Mayor was because he'd become bored with the position.

These days, he liked to wield his power from behind the scenes, from the shadows. The current Mayor owed his job to Kurt Remarque, and my own boss, Police Chief Carey, was a personal friend of Kurt's.

I grabbed my coat, and headed for the door.

3
KURT REMARQUE

I was in a hurry, so I decided to take the Main Gutter Line most of the way. It was a bit further, but it was faster, so …

But wait a minute. You have no idea what the Main Gutter Line is, do you?

Of course not. You monkey people can't see what's right in front of your faces most of the time. You charge around town in your cars and buses, on your bikes and on your trains, and you think that's the **only** way to do things.

Well, let me tell you, rats have been making their way across town for years, and most of the time you have absolutely no idea we're even here. Typical.

Let me give you an example. Let's say I need to stock up on a few supplies from the supermarket. Easy. There's a small trapdoor in the basement of my house, and that leads into the Sewer Walk that runs across town. Four hundred metres south of my place on the Sewer Walk I take a left-hand turn down Branch Line

Four, and a right turn two hundred metres after that. The fourth shaft along leads me up into the warehouse cellar, which is full of boxes. Boxes of toilet paper, stacked right to the ceiling — toilet paper boxes that are about to be delivered to ... **the supermarket**.

An enterprising rat like me simply hops into one of the boxes closest to the door (tossing the odd toilet roll off into the corner to make room), makes himself comfortable, and waits a few minutes.

Before too long a truck arrives (there's one every five minutes, twenty-four hours a day, seven days a week), loads up the box, and I'm on my way to the supermarket loading dock.

Rat shopping paradise! Out of the box, up and down the aisles (discreetly, of course), gathering whatever I need. Bread, biscuits, chocolates. Some rats go straight for the cheese, but personally I hate the stuff. Give me a good doughnut any day.

With my shopping organised, I head back to the loading dock, jump into one of the empty boxes, and settle back to wait. Thank goodness for recycling! Within a few minutes the box, with me inside it, is on its way back to the warehouse to be reused. Easy!

But today was not a shopping day. Today I was going to see Kurt Remarque, and I was in a hurry.

I left my office, slipped into the wall cavity that ran down the side of the disused factory, jumped through a grate into the stormwater drain that ran under the main road, and emerged on the other side. From there, I dashed up the nearest drainpipe like a rat up a drainpipe, and emerged on the roof of a long set of terrace houses that ran beside the main street all the way into town.

This was the Main Gutter Line, and a rat on the move could follow it for kilometres — which is exactly what I did right now.

But all good things must come to an end, so after a few minutes I slipped back down a convenient drainpipe and emerged at the main road again.

Now, to get to Kurt Remarque's office from here, I would normally head back down into the Sewer Walk, under the road, into the air vent of a disused air conditioner, underneath the dry-cleaning shop and out through a broken tile into the alleyway. But today I was in a hurry, and it looked quiet on the street, so I chanced it. With a quick glance in both directions, I dashed straight across the main road in the direction of the alley.

The woman on the bicycle was moving surprisingly fast for someone that old. She was pretty quiet, too. The first thing I knew, she was almost on top of me, a flash of metal and rubber coming fast from my left. She must have seen me about the same time I saw her, judging by the reaction.

'EeeeeeeeeK! A rat!'

I ducked my head and darted across into the safety of the dark, dank alley as speedily as I could. Behind me I heard the skidding of tyres and the screeching of the old lady as she bounced off a lamppost, careened into the side of a parked car, then collapsed in the gutter in a heap.

Monkey people! What on earth are they afraid of?

I slipped down the alley and away from the scene of the accident, keeping to the shadows as much as I could.

Kurt Remarque's place was right down the end, between two old rubbish bins and a dumpster. Not the best neighbourhood, you might think, but we rats don't put too much store in appearances.

As I approached the two bins, I heard a noise like a motor softly running. A quiet, menacing motor. It was like a purring sound. In fact, come to think of it, it **was** a purring sound.

Out from behind the bins came a **HUGE ginger cat**, its yellow eyes glaring at me. The fur on its back began to stand on end and it arched its back as its purring turned into a snarling, spitting sound.

I took two steps forward and slapped the metal bin hard with my hand. 'Get off out of here!' I yelled, and the cat turned tail and shot through, moving faster than an old lady on a bicycle.

One thing you have to understand about cats: they're essentially cowards. Any rat worth his cheese can usually chase off a cat four times his size. It's mice who have the most to fear from cats, and as far as I'm concerned, mice and cats deserve each other.

I skirted round the bins, slipped behind the dumpster and found the small green door set into the brick wall at the end of the alley. I knocked loudly three times, and waited.

The door was opened almost immediately by a tall, thin rat dressed in a grey topcoat. He looked down his long nose at me. Not that he had much choice, to be fair. After all, he was almost twice my height.

'This way, Inspector,' he said in a low whisper. 'Mr Remarque is expecting you.'

I followed him down a long corridor, treading on thick red carpet all the way. At the end was another green door. Mr 'I'm So Tall I Have to Look Down on You' touched the door twice with his knuckles. It wasn't so much a knock as a caress.

'Come.'

The voice was deep and gruff. The voice of Kurt Remarque.

'He'll see you now,' said the tall rat, rather unnecessarily.

I edged past him and walked into the room.

Kurt Remarque was sitting behind a huge mahogany desk, studying a sheaf of papers and ignoring me completely.

No matter how many times I see Kurt Remarque, I'm always amazed at his appearance.

He's a big rat, tall and wide and thick. He always wears a heavy black suit, a crisp white shirt and a bright red tie.

But if his suit is the blackest of blacks, his fur is the whitest of whites. And you understand why when he removes the black sunglasses he always wears to reveal a pair of watery pale pink eyes.

You see, Kurt Remarque is an albino rat — a very rare thing indeed. His white fur makes him look as soft and gentle as Father Christmas, but his pale pink eyes are cold and hard, and they can stare right through you.

He lifted those pink eyes now from the papers he was reading, and looked right through me.

'Ah, Inspector O'Malley,' he said. A warm smile lit up his mouth and made his whiskers twitch, but petered out long before it reached those eyes. 'Sit down, sit down.'

I took a seat in front of his desk and waited to see what he wanted.

After pretending to look through those papers once more, Kurt Remarque finally set them down and turned his attention fully to me.

'Now, I understand you're looking into an explosion — an explosion at a cheese factory.'

'Yes, indeed,' I said, wondering to myself how on earth he knew this.

'That cheese factory is one of mine, you know.'

I didn't know, and said so. But to be honest, it didn't really surprise me. Kurt Remarque owned half the city, after all, so it stood to reason that there were quite a few factories among his possessions.

'So ...' He leant forward and fixed me with his pale, watery stare. 'What have you found?'

'Well, it's only early days yet,' I replied, 'but the investigation is going very well. In fact, we've already ...'

Kurt Remarque shook his head impatiently, interrupting me.

'No, I don't mean how is the investigation going. I mean precisely what I said. What have you **found?**'

'I don't understand. We've found lots of melted cheese, broken furniture ...'

'You didn't find anything ... *interesting?*'

'Well, the melted blue cheese was fairly interesting. It went into swirls, like blueberry ice cream ...'

'Not the **cheese**, Inspector, forget the **cheese**!' Kurt Remarque sighed, and leant even further forward in his chair. 'Did you find anything else? Anything **unusual?**'

I sat back in my chair and scratched my chin.

Now, I haven't been a detective these past ten years for nothing. I know when something is suspicious, and this was VERY suspicious.

What on earth was Kurt Remarque on about?

'No, nothing unusual at all,' I replied.

Kurt Remarque leant back in his chair, just as I had leant back in mine. He studied me carefully.

'So,' he said briskly, as if he were changing the subject, 'how is the investigation going, then? Any clues? Any breakthroughs?'

Something inside me told me this was not the time to mention the mouse footprint, or the River Road Mouse Gang. I had no idea what was on Kurt Remarque's mind, so why should I tell him what was on mine?

'Not really,' I said, as casually as I could. 'But we're right onto the case, Mr Remarque. I'm sure we'll turn up something in no time at all.'

'Well, keep me posted, O'Malley. Keep me posted. Soon as something breaks, there's a good chap.'

He looked down to his papers again, and I knew I was dismissed.

As I made my way back along the Main Gutter Line I was deep in thought.

Why was Kurt Remarque so interested in the fire? Sure, it was in one of his factories, but he had plenty of those. And why did he keep talking about something **interesting?**

By the time I slipped back down the wall cavity to my office I had made up my mind.

I needed to go back to the scene of the crime, and I needed to go alone.

Imagine a dark, cold, lonely street. Deserted. The only sound is the soft shuffle of feet on the pavement.

Rat feet. **My** feet.

It was almost midnight as I drew close to the burnt-out, ruined entrance to Kurt Remarque's cheese factory. The door had been boarded up, of course, by

members of my highly efficient police force, and there was bright orange tape stretched from side to side of the doorway. **CRIME SCENE! DO NOT ENTER** was written across the tape in bold black letters.

It takes more than that to stop Octavius O'Malley. I knew that the secret to tonight's impromptu examination was to gain access to the scene discreetly and leave no sign that I had even been there, so I proceeded carefully.

First, I bent down under the tape, delicately squeezing my body in between the tape and the boarded-up door. Then I began to prize off one of the wooden planks that had been nailed roughly across the half-burnt door. Placing the plank carefully on the ground behind me, I began to prize off a second. That would give me enough room to slip through into the factory storeroom, and see what I would see.

The middle two planks had now been removed. I pushed open the blackened door and stepped gingerly over the third plank, still nailed across the doorway at about knee-height. (That's knee-height for a rat, of course. Knee-height for a human and I'd need a ladder.)

Have I mentioned how slippery melted cheese is? And how hard it is to see in the dark? Well, if I haven't, take my word for it. I put my left leg over the plank and stepped straight onto a particularly greasy mound of what felt like edam cheese. (I have a good feel for these things.) My leg shot out from under me and I dropped heavily onto the plank, with one leg on either side of it.

The plank gave way under my weight and I fell backwards into the orange tape. It stretched back like a rubber band, then fired me into the room like a slingshot.

There was a crash, a splinter of wood, and a sort of splodgy sound as I bounced off a broken chair and landed in more cheese.

So much for my discreet entrance.

I stood up, wiped myself down, felt for bruises and then looked around. I could see ... **nothing**.

It was at about this moment that I realised I probably should have brought a torch with me.

'Yes, what we need is a little light on the subject,' I muttered to myself, and at that precise instant a powerful shaft of light burst across the room, hitting me right in the face.

'Just what do you think you're doing?' came a high-pitched, screeching voice from somewhere behind the light. 'I'll have the police onto you!'

'I **am** the police!' I said indignantly. 'Now, take that light away from my face this second!'

The angle of the light shifted towards the ground and came a little nearer. Now I could see that it belonged to a torch, and that the torch belonged to a hunched, grey-whiskered rat, who was limping and stooping his way towards me.

'I might have known,' complained the old rat in his screechy, scratchy voice. 'I'm up half the night with the fire, then I'm pestered all day with **stupid** questions from stupid police, and then I'm woken up tonight by **more** stupid police stumbling around where they shouldn't be!'

'Never mind that, old rat,' I said with what I imagined was quiet dignity. 'I am Inspector Octavius O'Malley, and I am in charge of this investigation. I have every right to be here. And who might you be?'

'Well, I **might** be anybody,' said the old rat, holding the torch up to his face so I could get a good look at his wrinkly nose and squinting eyes. 'I **might** be the

devil himself, mightn't I, for all you know. Fact is, I'm not. Fact is, I'm Boskin, and I'm what passes for a caretaker round here.'

He came a little closer and peered at me. 'What are you doing here, anyway? This time of night, making all this racket?'

'I am investigating the scene of the crime.'

'In the dark?'

'I forgot my torch.'

This conversation wasn't going too well. I could see I would have to take charge of matters, or I would end up stuck here half the night talking to a cranky old caretaker.

'Now, what I would like to do, Mr Boskin,' I said firmly, 'is to borrow your torch for a little while so that I can make a few inspections.'

'**Would** you, now?' snapped Boskin, grasping his torch firmly with both hands. 'Well, well, would you indeed? Do you know what **I'd** like to do? Do you even **care** what I'd like to do?'

I sighed. 'What would you like to do, Boskin?'

'**I'd like to get some sleep!**' screeched Boskin. 'If I'm going to spend the next few weeks cleaning up this cheese-coated mess, working my tail off to put things right for Mr Remarque, then right now, since it's the middle of the night, **I'd like to get some sleep!**'

He thrust the torch into my hands, turned on his heels and shuffled off into the darkness. He was surprisingly quick for an old rat, and how he managed to walk in the dark without bumping into things I'll never know.

Just as he had been almost swallowed up by the darkness, he stopped and turned back to me. I could just make out the shadows of his face, and his voice was faint, like a shrill whisper.

'Look carefully, Inspector. That's my advice. Look carefully.'

'Why do you say that?' I half-yelled across the darkness.

The shrill, soft whisper came back to me.

'There's something ... not quite right about this place. Something ... funny. Supposed to be a simple little cheese factory, but there are people who come here. **Important** people. Mr Remarque and his friends. Lots of coming and going. Lots of talking. Precious little cheese-making, from what I can see. And tell me, what does an important man like Mr Remarque want to be coming down to this little cheese factory all the time for? Better things to do with his time, I would have thought. I tell you, something is just … not right. You check **that** out with your torch and your big feet!'

'Did you tell that to the other police today?' I asked.

'Those whippersnappers!' said Boskin a little more loudly. 'Hah! What do they care about what an old caretaker thinks? Who has the keys to this place — that's all they cared about. Who has the keys, was the door locked, did you smell smoke? Never mind all that nonsense. You just see if I'm not right.'

And with that he limped off into the night, heading for whatever shack he slept in, and I turned back into the room to start my secret midnight search.

I spent two hours in that cheesy mess, pointing Boskin's torch in all directions, looking for clues.

The mouse-print was long gone, scraped up and taken away by Sergeant Smith, and there seemed to be nothing else worth worrying about. Nothing but a slimy tide of cheese: cheddar in one corner, soft camembert and brie smeared up one wall, and a large stinky swamp of blue and green gorgonzola oozing out from a huge bent cheese tin in the centre of the room.

'There must be **something**,' I said aloud to myself as I scoured the room. Why else would Kurt Remarque be so keen to know if I'd found anything? And what was that crazy old caretaker going on and on about?

Finally, frustrated and tired, I turned to go.

It was a pity about that table leg sticking out from a mound of cheese.

I walked straight into it, of course, dropped the torch, slipped backwards, bounced off a wall and slammed face-first into the cheese tin in the middle of the room. It rang like a bell.

'That's not right, Ocko,' I muttered to myself as I reached around for the torch. 'That hurt way too much.'

I found the torch in the gorgonzola slime, switched it on and took a closer look at the sheet of metal I'd landed against. It was far too thick and heavy to be part of a cheese tin. It must have been several centimetres thick, and it had a small circular handle set into one end. It looked for all the world like …

'A trapdoor!' I yelled aloud into the echoing darkness. 'A solid steel trapdoor!'

But what was it for? And what was under it?

Setting the torch down carefully in the cheesy mess, I braced myself, grabbed the circular handle, and pulled.

It wouldn't budge. It was bent in the middle so that

it looked like the roof of a house, and all around the edges the melted cheese had fixed it in place like glue.

Hmmmm … My superbly honed, highly experienced investigative instincts took over. This didn't smell right — and I wasn't just talking about the cheese.

Luckily, I like a challenge.

I picked up the chunk of table leg that had knocked me over in the first place, and spent almost an hour digging and scraping away the cheesy glue. Then I braced myself and pulled with all my strength against the metal trapdoor.

It rocked, it groaned, it slid a few centimetres, then it toppled over into the cheesy mess. Of course, I toppled over too.

I sat up, sweating a little, and shone the torch on my handiwork.

There, cut into the floorboards in the middle of the room, was a neat, square hole. It was about the same size as the steel trapdoor I'd hauled out of the way.

Now, being a fairly ignorant monkey person (no offence), you probably can't work out what that means. But to a seasoned investigative rat like me, it was obvious.

A secret compartment.

The River Road Mouse Gang had been after whatever was in this secret compartment. They had blown up the whole room just to open it and steal whatever was inside.

I stared down at the compartment that had been revealed. The bottom and the sides were solid steel. They were a little blackened in a few spots, but otherwise the secret compartment was in pretty good shape.

Oh, there's probably one more thing I should mention ... **It was empty.**

Of course it was empty! How silly do you think I am?

Did you really expect the famous River Road Mouse Gang to break into a cheese factory, blow up the storeroom, open a secret compartment then leave empty-handed?

I dragged the sheet of metal back into place and shoved a few lumps of cheese and scraps of wood over the top. For now, this would be my little secret — until I could go back for another word with Kurt Remarque.

I left the factory, knocking the two planks back into place across the door with the old caretaker's torch. I would have to return it to him, but where was he?

'There must be a shack or a shed around here somewhere,' I thought, as I slipped carefully under the police tape.

Just then I heard footsteps behind me. 'Ah,' I thought, 'this must be Boskin coming back to retrieve his torch.' I wondered if he knew about the secret compartment, and what was kept in it. Money? Jewels? Gold?

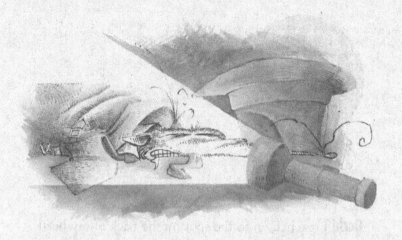

I was about to turn in the direction of the footsteps when something very, very hard bopped me on the head. I fell to the ground unconscious, just like they do in the movies.

5
THE GANG IS REVEALED

Ouch! I reached up to the spot on the back of my head that hurt so much and rubbed it. Now it hurt even more.

Blearily, I opened my eyes and looked around. Four walls, a floor and a roof. One door, no windows. I had no idea where I was, but it looked like some sort of prison cell. I tried to sit up and a wave of dizziness washed over me. I was lying on a bed, and beside it was a chair, but otherwise the room was empty.

'Well,' I thought to myself, 'someone is in a whole lot of trouble. Attacking and kidnapping an Inspector of Police!'

After a while I started to feel a little better, so I got up slowly from the bed and walked over to the door. It was a very solid wooden door, and it was locked. But there is one thing that can get through a locked door, and that's sound.

So I yelled.

'Oi! Who's out there? What's going on? You're in a

lot of trouble, you know, a lot of trouble! Do you have any idea who I am?'

There was no answer, and I couldn't think of anything else to say, so I sat down on the bed again and waited.

Someone must have heard me, though, because a few minutes later I heard the rattling sound of a lock being released, then the door flew open.

Standing in the doorway was a mouse. A small, insignificant-looking mouse wearing a red waistcoat, green trousers and thick, dark sunglasses.

'Who are you?' I demanded, standing up quickly.

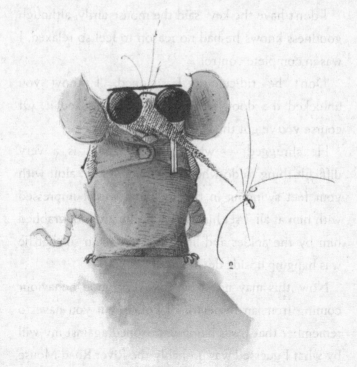

The small mouse ignored me. Instead of replying, he darted into the room, slammed the door and relocked it behind him. With that chore done, he strolled casually into the centre of the room, and looked me slowly up and down.

'I see you're awake,' he squeaked.

I was in no mood for pleasantries. With one swift movement, I grabbed the little squirt under both arms and lifted him off the ground. He was now at eye-level with me, and his tiny legs dangled in the air.

'I want the key,' I said gruffly. 'I'm getting out of here.'

'I don't have the key,' said the mouse airily, although goodness knows he had no reason to feel so relaxed. I was in complete control.

'Don't be ridiculous!' I snapped. 'I know you unlocked the door, and I know you relocked it. Of course you've got the key!'

He shrugged — which I must admit is a very difficult thing to do when you're being held aloft with your feet swinging in the air. But I wasn't impressed with him at all. I set him down on the ground, grabbed him by the ankles and lifted him up again so that he was hanging upside down.

Now, this may not seem like very good behaviour coming from an Inspector of Police, but you have to remember that I was being imprisoned against my will by what I guessed was probably the River Road Mouse

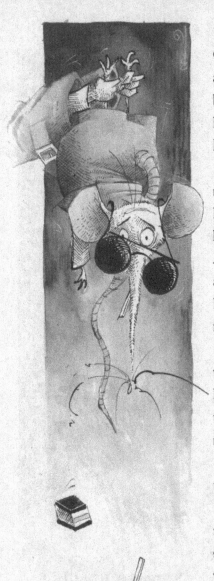

Gang. I was tired and cold and hungry, and I had a bump on the back of my head the size of a lemon. Besides, this was **fun**.

I shook that little mouse up and down as hard as I could, but no key fell out of his pockets. A packet of chewing gum, a toothpick and a piece of liquorice dropped to the floor, but no key.

Just as I was wondering where on earth he had hidden it, I heard the lock turn once more behind me.

'I see you've met Patrick the Magnificent.'

I put the mouse down reluctantly and turned to see who my latest visitor was.

It was another mouse.

A tall, thin mouse with luxuriant black fur, leaning casually against the doorframe. This mouse was also wearing a red waistcoat and green trousers, but was very easy to distinguish from the other mouse because of being so much taller. Oh yes, and because of being a female mouse.

(**So how do you know it was a female mouse?** I can hear you asking. **Don't they all look the same?** Well, to a monkey person, maybe they do. But to a fellow rodent, there's an enormous difference. The twinkle in the eyes, the length of the whiskers, the curve of the hips, the way they stand. Trust me, this was a female mouse.)

'Allow me to introduce myself,' she said, slinking into the room with her hand outstretched. 'My name is Spencer, and if you haven't already guessed, I am the leader of the River Road Mouse Gang.'

Well, you could have blown me down with a feather. At least I **imagine** you could have blown me down with a feather, but since no one had a feather as far as I could see, we'll never know, will we?

I had finally met my nemesis, my arch enemy, my dastardly foe — and it was a **girl**. I can't explain why, but it was the last thing I expected. But I wasn't about to let them know I'd been caught unawares, so I snapped into action with a quick retort.

'Um …' I said.

'You'd better sit down, Inspector,' returned Spencer,

closing the door and coming to sit down on the chair next to the bed. 'I have a lot to tell you.'

I glanced over her shoulder to the door, and it was as if she read my mind.

'Don't bother about trying to escape,' she added. The rest of the gang are outside. You won't get far. Patrick the Magnificent only locked the door in the first place as a precaution, because most of us were still asleep.'

I sat down on the edge of the bed. I was beginning to regain my composure.

'By the way,' I asked casually, 'how did the little guy lock the door anyway? I checked him for a key, and he didn't have one.'

Spencer laughed. 'Oh, Patrick the Magnificent doesn't need a key. He can open just about any lock with nothing more than a toothpick and a piece of chewing gum.'

Of course.

'And what about the liquorice?' I said.

'What **about** the liquorice?'

'What does he do with a piece of liquorice?'

Spencer looked at me as if I were an idiot.

'Well, I imagine he eats it,' she said after a moment. 'It tastes quite nice, you know. Anyway, can we stop talking about liquorice now? I have some very important things to tell you, and we don't have much time.'

'Don't talk to me like that!' I snapped back, in my best official Inspector of Police voice. 'You're under arrest!'

'Yes, well let's put all that to one side, shall we, and move on?' said Spencer. 'What do you know about the explosion at the cheese factory?'

'Not as much as I'd like to know, but I'd bet my whiskers it was your gang that was behind it all.'

'Well, you'd be right.'

'Oh, so you admit it?' I said triumphantly.

'Yes, we did it,' answered Spencer airily. 'We heard a rumour that Kurt Remarque was spending rather a lot of time at one particular factory of his, and taking a lot of other important rats with him.'

'Like who?'

'Like the Mayor,' Spencer replied. 'Like your own Chief of Police, and half the businessrats in town.'

I frowned as I sat there listening. **What was this all about?**

Spencer was still talking.

'... so anyway, given all that strange activity, the gang thought it was high time we paid a visit to the cheese factory, to see what was so special about it.'

'And blow it up?'

'Well, we didn't really mean to do that. Pat the Magnificent got us in with no problems, and it didn't take us long to find that secret compartment in the floor under the table. They don't call us the best criminal gang in town for nothing, after all. But no matter what he tried, Pat couldn't get that stupid thing open.'

The little mouse in the dark glasses interrupted Spencer's story.

'I would've got it eventually, I know I would! A few more minutes and an extra piece of wire, and I would have opened it. No lock will ever beat me! Ever!'

'Be that as it may,' said Spencer patiently, 'we gave Pat half an hour, and we couldn't waste any more time on it. So we blew it.'

'That's the understatement of the year,' I said. 'You blew up half the factory!'

Spencer looked a bit sheepish — which is not easy for a mouse.

'Yes, well, we did rather overdo the dynamite, I grant you that. But it did the trick. It blew open one side of the trapdoor, so we levered it open and made off with the contents as fast we could. That horrible cheese slowed us down a bit, but we still got out of there lickety-split.'

'So don't keep me in suspense,' I said. 'What was in there? What did you steal? Money? Jewels? Gold?'

'No.' Spencer got up and walked over to the door. She knocked twice, and twice again. Someone opened the door from the other side and handed through a dusty cardboard box, which Spencer carried back to me. The door slammed shut again. 'Gold or jewels was what I was expecting, too,' she said. 'What I wasn't expecting was … **this!**

Spencer dropped the box in my lap with a flourish, turned on her heel and left. Patrick the Magnificent followed her, closing the door behind him.

I was left alone in the tiny cell once more, with a heavy cardboard box in my lap.

6
THE EVIL PLAN OF KURT REMARQUE

The lid of the box came off easily enough.

I looked inside.

It contained a book.

'Is **that** all?' I said to myself. 'Is that what all this fuss is about? The explosion, the robbery, my kidnapping, Kurt Remarque's strange behaviour? All for some measly **book?**'

I picked up the book and put the box to one side. It was a big book, with heavy leather binding.

As soon as I opened the front cover, I could see it wasn't a proper, printed book. It was more like a diary, or a collection of handwritten notes.

The writing changed as I flicked through the pages, but I recognised the first lot of handwriting immediately. It was a broad, flowing style: unmistakably script of Kurt Remarque himself.

I turned back to the first page, made myself as comfortable as I could, and began to read.

I have decided that it is important to History that I keep some form of record of the remarkable events that are about to unfold.

Be assured that these words have been written down by none other than Kurt Remarque, a name that will live in History as a leader of rats, a setter of destinies, a maker of new worlds and new realities.

When future generations come to read of my magnificent plan, and the way in which I have brought it into being, they will understand at last that I stand above all other rats.

For hundreds of years, as long as rodent memory can reach, mankind has persecuted rats. They have trapped us, chased us, poisoned us and reviled us. They have set dogs upon us; they have set cats upon us.

When they built their huge, overcrowded cities, the Plague was visited upon them. And they blamed us for the Plague. It was their dirt, their filth and their disease, but it was our fault.

Since those times, rats have been forced into the darkness and the shadows, chased and hated by generation after generation of humans.

And now, here in our own city, a new plan has been formed to rid the town of rats once and for all. The humans of this town have offered a prize of ten million dollars to anyone who can kill all the rats who live here. Like Saint Patrick drove the snakes out of Ireland, our human city fathers are determined to drive all the rats out of our city. They want a modern-day Pied Piper to lead the rats out of our very own Hamelin.

And they will have it.

They will have it, because I will give it to them. Kurt Remarque will provide the means whereby the last rat will be driven out of our town.

And then, my friends, then a new day will begin.

I beg your pardon? **Excuse me?** Am I going mad?

I don't usually ask myself three questions in a row, but then again I don't usually open up a book and read that the most important rat in town has come up with a plan to destroy all rats.

What on earth had Kurt Remarque been drinking?

I had got to the end of the first page of the book, so I turned over. The next page contained some sort of advertisement, or flyer, that had been stuck into the book. I quickly scanned it.

MUNICIPAL RAT ANNOUNCEMENT

The City Fathers hereby declare that a resolution has been passed allowing for the awarding of a **SUBSTANTIAL PRIZE** to anyone who devises a plan for the total elimination of the city's rats.

Such plan must be submitted to the Full Council for approval as soon as possible.

The successful plan will be implemented, and proof of success will be determined by an absence of rats in **ANY** part of town for at least six weeks after the completion of the plan.

If, after that time, our inspectors confirm that all rats have been destroyed or left the town's environs, a prize in the amount of **$10,000,000** will be duly awarded.

It is envisaged that the elimination of all rats will be a boon to mankind, leading to a cleaner and safer environment where once again the townsfolk can walk in peace and tranquillity.

It will also lead to a substantial increase in the manufacture of cat food, which will create an estimated 100 new local jobs.

All plans should be submitted to Hiram Grockle in the City Clerk's Office on foolscap paper in unmarked brown envelopes.

We regret that unsuccessful submissions cannot be returned.

So there really **was** a plan! Kurt Remarque had obviously gone stark raving mad, but the entire thing wasn't just a product of his twisted imagination.

It was bad enough that someone in the City Council had decided to launch an attack on the rat population. Bad, but hardly surprising. Kurt was right about one thing. You monkey people have always had it in for rodents.

What was surprising was that Kurt had somehow decided that this was a great idea, and that he was just the rat to bring it about.

It made no sense. No sense at all.

I turned the page of the book on my lap. The next page looked like the minutes of a meeting. I settled back with a mounting sense of dread, and read on.

Meeting Number 1, Cheese Factory Storeroom

*(Minutes prepared by Percival Pelliphant,
personal assistant to Mr Kurt Remarque)*

PRESENT:

KR; MAYOR MOTTLEY; POLICE CHIEF CAREY; ASSORTED
BUSINESSRATS AND PROMINENT RODENTS OF THE CITY; PP.

6.00 pm: KR opened the meeting by tabling a copy of the
confidential municipal announcement that had
come into his possession. General discussion of
an extremely animated nature followed.

6.57 pm: KR advised everyone to 'shut up and settle
down'.

7.08 pm: Mayor Mottley recommended emergency plan
be instituted. Police Chief Carey agreed.
KR advised Mayor and Police Chief they were
idiots. Further animated discussion.

7.43 pm: KR once again took the floor. He expressed the
view that any attempt on the part of the Mayor
and the rat police to defend the rodent
population was unlikely to succeed. Mayor
Mottley asked what choice they had. Police

Chief Carey added that any plan they devised was better than doing nothing. KR said there was a better way, and was asked to explain.

7.59 pm: KR explained. At the request of Mr Remarque, I, Percival Pelliphant, have transcribed in full the following speech by Mr Remarque to the first meeting of the select few in the Cheese Storeroom, being as it is a document of great historic importance.

SPEECH OF KURT REMARQUE
TO FIRST MEETING:

Gentlerats, we stand at a moment in history that will determine our very survival. For generations, mankind has sought to destroy the world of rats. This we know. What we now also know is that, in our own part of the world, the attempt to destroy rats has entered a new, more dangerous phase.

This document I have shown you today [and here Mr Remarque held aloft the municipal announcement] *makes it clear once and for all that the monkey people mean business. Ten million dollars, gentlerats. Ten million dollars! What wouldn't a greedy human do for ten million dollars? What wouldn't any of us do for ten million dollars?*

'So, what's to be done?' I hear you cry. 'Just give up? Allow ourselves to be exterminated? Flee the city in disgrace and humiliation?' Never! Never!

I have a plan.

Of course I have a plan. I am Kurt Remarque. I have built Rodent City up into the model of civic virtue that it is today. And I tell you gentlerats assembled here that I will not see it destroyed.

Let the foolish monkey men have their competition. Let them trawl far and wide for a plan to eliminate us rats. Let them think they are taking charge of the situation; let them think they are doing something. All the while, there will only be one who is doing

something, one who is in charge. And that will be …
Kurt Remarque.

Don't you see? The only way we can turn this
ridiculous competition to our advantage is … to win it
ourselves!

We must devise the best plan to rid the city of rats,
and then make sure it wins the competition. Needless to
say, the lives of some rats, perhaps many rats, will be lost.
Collateral damage, I am afraid to say. But by controlling
the situation and the timing of the plan, we can ensure
that a small group of survivors will live on. Those
survivors — including, may I add, all those present in
this room — need only lay low for six weeks and then
we can return and rebuild. Slowly at first, but we shall
eventually restore Rodent City to its former glory. In
fact, I believe we can make it better than ever — a centre
of excellence for elite rats. And we can do this, my fellow
rodents, with ten million dollars in start-up capital.
Think of what we can achieve! With funds like that,
nothing can stop us! We can finally be what we have
always been destined to become — the finest city of rats
the world has ever known!

****

8.16 pm: KR resumed his seat after the speech. All eyes
were on him, but no one spoke for almost a
minute.

8.17 pm: Mayor Mottley broke the silence by asking how
KR could ensure that his plan was the one

chosen. KR replied that this would be quite
simple: their plan would be the best. It would be
a simple plan to flood the city with rat poison,
but it would have one thing that no other plan
possessed. It would have . . . THE MAP.

****

There were more notes on the following pages, from
later meetings, but I couldn't read on. I closed the
book again, more shocked than I could ever remember
being in all my years as a policerat.

Kurt Remarque was going to reveal the one thing
that had always been jealously guarded. The one thing
that had been protected for all time from falling into
the hands of humans. He was going to reveal ...
THE MAP.

8

THE MAP

I suppose you want to know what the map is, and why it's so important. Well, it's not that hard to work out when you think about it.

I've already told you about the Sewer Walk — remember Chapter 3? Pay attention!

There are sewers and gutter lines and hollow walls and crevices and tunnels all over the city. There are covered laneways and pipes and hidden ladders. It's all part of an elaborate series of ratways built up over many years to help us get around town without being bothered by you monkey people. Every rat community has access to a pathway of some sort; every home is connected to the system.

Now, we used to carry all of this information around in our heads for years. When I was a young rat, Rodent City was still fairly small. Everyone knew each other, and everyone was taught the paths and thoroughfares through town.

But as time passed and the city grew ever larger, this became impractical. Soon there were hundreds of pathways and tunnels crisscrossing the city, and there was no way to remember them all.

It was back in the days when Kurt Remarque was Mayor that the idea of a map first came up. Soon the idea became a reality. A small leather-bound directory was produced, showing the exact location of every tunnel and gutter in Rodent City.

It was the only book any rat had ever produced, and each copy was numbered and jealously guarded, lest it fall into the hands of the humans. That little book told the story of our rodent community; it was a master guide of where we all lived and worked and travelled each day.

And now, Kurt Remarque was going to hand over this most treasured document to the monkey people, knowing that they would use it to destroy us.

'You fool! You'll never get away with it!' I yelled out loud to the empty room, the book ignored for the moment on my lap. 'You've forgotten about the great Ocko! I'll stop you, you tyrant. Just wait until the Police Chief hears about this. He'll —'

I stopped in mid-speech, suddenly remembering. Police Chief Carey had been sitting in the meeting with Kurt Remarque. He already knew all about it. Did that make him part of the conspiracy? Was he going along with this dastardly plan?

I picked up the book to read on, but as I did so the cell door opened and Spencer sauntered back in.

'I heard you call out from down the hall. Did you want something? Have you finished reading?'

I could only stare at her and blurt out the first thing that came into my head.

'He's giving them **THE MAP!**'

'Ah,' said Spencer, 'I see you've got that far. Now perhaps you can see what we're dealing with.'

'But it's monstrous! We must stop it!' I cried.

'Yes, but how?' said Spencer, moving over to sit near me on the chair. 'After all, it's not just Kurt Remarque who's dreamt this up. The Mayor's involved, and the Police Chief — your own boss.'

'Are you sure?' I asked uncertainly. 'I know Police Chief Carey was at the first meeting, I've read that far. But I can't believe he'd go along with this madness.'

'Well, believe it,' said the mouse, snatching the book from my lap and leafing through the pages. 'There are another five meetings described in this book, and Carey and the Mayor are at all of them. According to these minutes, they ask questions, they discuss the details, they even suggest a few ideas. As far as I can see, they're all in this thing together.'

'But I don't understand,' I said. 'How on earth are they going to present their plan to the city and win the right to carry out the contract? What human in their right mind would hire a bunch of **rats** to eliminate **rats**?'

'Ah,' said Spencer, 'I see you haven't got that far.' She licked her tiny paw and turned over a couple of pages. 'Here,' she said, pointing to a paragraph halfway down the last page of the minutes. 'Read this.'

****

9.25 pm: Mayor Mottley asked KR how the plan and the Map were to be submitted to the humans. KR replied that there was only one way: human partners needed to be enlisted to the plot. Discussion on the dangers of dealing with humans. How could monkey people be trusted?

9.40 pm: KR replied that, once again, he had thought of everything. The plan would work if the right humans were chosen. They needed to be experienced in pest control and credible enough to look the part. However, they also needed to be stupid enough to be easily manipulated and controlled, and desperate enough to agree to work with rats. Police Chief Carey asked where they would find these humans, who were experienced, credible, stupid AND desperate. KR advised the meeting not to worry — he had found them already. They would be attending the very next meeting.

****

'Who?' I asked Spencer. 'Who are they going to use?'

'Don't ask me,' said Spencer. 'I may be brilliant, but I'm not that brilliant. I only know what I've read in those minutes, just like you. If we want to know who the humans are, then we'll just have to find out, won't we?'

'Wait a minute,' I said suspiciously, getting to my feet. 'What do you mean **we? We** aren't going to do anything. There **are** no we. I'm a Police Inspector, and you're the leader of a gang of criminals. Criminal **mice**, for heaven's sake. All I'm going to do is arrest you for malicious damage, theft, assault, kidnapping —'

'Oh, wake up to yourself, O'Malley!' snapped Spencer, getting to her feet as well. 'This is the biggest crime in the history of Rodent City. Who are you going to turn to? Who can you trust? Your own Police Chief is part of the plot.'

'And you think I should turn to **you?**' I snarled. 'A gang of criminal mice?'

Spencer fixed her blue eyes on me with a steely stare.

'There's no one else,' she said quietly. 'Look, O'Malley, I don't like it any more than you do. I hate rats. All rats. You've been oppressing us for years. You hate the way the monkey people treat **you**, and then you turn around and treat **us** the same way! If I could think of how to make this problem go away without turning to a dirty rat, then believe me, I would. But you can be sure of one thing. If Kurt Remarque gets his way, the streets and gutters and tunnels of Rodent City will be awash with rat poison, and that won't just kill all the rats, it will kill all the mice too. My fellow mice and I will be the innocent victims of this plot as much as you will, and I'm not about to let that happen. I figure we're in this together, whether we like it or not. So why not turn on that so-called brilliant brain of yours, and come up with a plan, fast? Because right now, I'm all out of ideas.'

Spencer sat back down on the chair, folded her arms and glared at me, her whiskers twitching.

It was the longest speech I'd ever heard from a mouse. It was rude and disrespectful and ... true. I hated to admit it to myself, but she was right.

To think that it had come to this! Rats working with humans to destroy Rodent City, and now I, Octavius O'Malley, had to work with mice to defeat them. **Could things get any worse?**

Well, I suppose if I failed, and the streets were flooded with poison, that would definitely be worse.

Did I have a choice? No, I did not.

I looked at Spencer, who was looking back at me.

'Well,' I said briskly. 'We'd better get along to that next meeting, and find out who those humans are.'

Spencer smiled a small smile, as if she'd won an important battle but didn't want to waste time gloating. Then she turned to business.

'Well, brilliant, O'Malley,' she said sarcastically. 'It doesn't take a genius to work **that** one out. Of course we need to spy on their next meeting, but how do we do that? Look at the minutes in the book! There's no dates mentioned, no times, nothing. We don't know exactly when those meetings were held, let alone when the next one will be. Or where, for that matter, now that the cheese factory has exploded.'

'First of all,' I said decisively, 'call me Ocko. Everyone else does. And second, I suggest we get moving. I have a plan.'

9
BOSKIN THE CARETAKER

I stepped out into the sunlight, followed by Spencer and Patrick the Magnificent — the only other member of the River Road Mouse Gang I had met so far.

As I squinted against the afternoon light, I looked around to get my bearings. We were in a narrow alley, surrounded on all sides by piles of rubbish. The door

we had come out of was a small, nondescript one, with the words **NO ENTRY** painted roughly across it. So this was the celebrated hideout of the River Road Mouse Gang! Just a few days ago I would have given my right whiskers to know where this hideout was, but now I hardly gave it a second thought. I was on the trail of something far more important.

'Where are we going?' Patrick the Magnificent asked Spencer.

'I have absolutely no idea,' she replied. 'Why don't you ask the Inspector? He seems to be leading the way.'

'Where are we going?' Patrick said again, this time to me.

'Shut up, mouse,' I said.

We walked to the end of the alley, turned left into a hollow wall, then climbed a length of fallen beam until we got to a section of the Main Gutter Line and I worked out my bearings.

We walked in silence. I could tell that Patrick the Magnificent was still sulking at the way I'd snapped at him, and Spencer was probably wondering whether she'd made the right decision in confiding in a rat. As for me, I was just hoping no one I knew saw me in the company of mice. What would **that** do for the reputation of Inspector Octavius O'Malley?

All in all, we were a sullen, preoccupied and silent group of rodents as we made our way through the streets.

After quite some time, I led us off the Main Gutter Line and stuck to the shadowy back streets for several blocks. Finally we turned a corner, and there was the familiar burnt-out building, the orange tape still spread across the doorway. Kurt Remarque's cheese factory.

'What do you think we'll find here?' asked Spencer.

'Not what,' I replied, 'but who.'

I led Spencer and Patrick round the outside of the building and into a dusty yard at the back.

'It must be here somewhere,' I muttered to myself.

We walked along the fence line, crossed through a back lane, then I spied a worn, rusty gateway on the other side. It creaked as I pushed it open and walked through into a second, smaller yard. This one was covered in clumps of ragged, yellowing grass, and in the far corner was a ramshackle shed. A wisp of smoke was rising from a tiny chimney on the roof.

'Aha,' I said.

'Aha?' said Spencer, raising one eyebrow and putting a paw on her hip. 'You mean to say police officers really **do** say "Aha" when they discover something? I thought that only happened in books or movies.'

I ignored her remark, strode across to the shed and rapped loudly on the door.

Nothing happened.

I knocked again, a little louder and longer.

Nothing happened.

'Come on Boskin, open up!' I demanded in my best police voice. 'I know you're in there!'

'Go away!' screeched a scratchy voice I'd heard before.

'Boskin?' said Patrick the Magnificent to me. 'Who's Boskin?'

'Shut up, mouse,' I said.

'I'm no mouse!' screeched Boskin from inside his shed.

'I wasn't talking to you, Boskin,' I yelled. 'Now, open up. It's the police.'

'Go away.'

'Oh, for goodness' sake!' I grumbled to myself. 'This could take all day.'

Before I could think of what to do next, that pesky little mouse walked up to the door, pulled a toothpick from his trouser pocket and stuck it into the lock on the shed door.

He jiggled it back and forth for a few seconds and the door popped open.

'Don't mention it,' said Patrick the Magnificent.

'I didn't,' I said.

'I know,' said Patrick.

'Shut up, mouse,' I snapped.

'Look,' said Spencer wearily, 'could we just get on with this? Rodent City is about to be destroyed and you two just want to argue. You sound like a bad stand-up comedy act.'

Ignoring her insult, I pushed open the door and strode into the shed. It was a tiny, one-room dwelling with a filthy looking bed in one corner, an even filthier looking sink in the other corner, and a table with one chair in the middle of the room.

Boskin was sitting on the chair with a small knife in his hand, peeling an onion. He glared balefully at me.

'Oh, it's **you!**' he screeched. 'Where's my torch, you thief?'

I could see this wasn't going to be easy.

'Now listen, Boskin ...' I began, but the old caretaker suddenly leapt to his feet, clambered onto the tabletop and began waving his knife around dangerously.

'Mice!' he squawked. 'Mice! You've brought filthy mice into my house!'

Spencer looked quite put out.

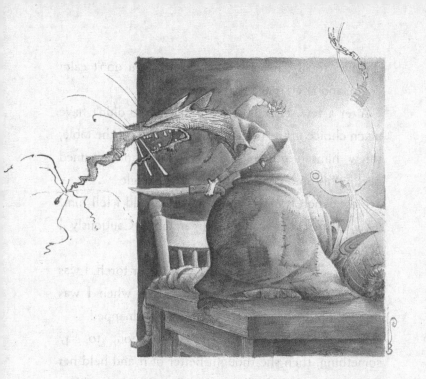

'I should think this house is quite filthy enough already,' she said smoothly. Then she turned to me. 'Look O'Malley, why don't you tell me why we're wasting our time with this old codger? Every minute is precious.'

Boskin froze, his knife still held at the ready.

'You **know** these vermin?' he spat. 'You mean to say you're travelling around with mice now? Is this what my tax dollars are being spent on? Police officers who hang around with mice, and steal torches to boot?'

'Now look, Boskin,' I said as patiently as I could, 'just get down off the table, eat your onion and let me explain. You'll burst a blood vessel if you don't calm down, and at your age that could be fatal.'

After a few seconds, Boskin realised he didn't have much choice in the matter, so he climbed off the table, threw himself grumpily into his seat and resumed peeling his onion, glaring at me all the while.

Now, where to start? How much should I tell him? Could I trust this grumpy old caretaker? Cautiously, I began.

'First of all, Boskin, I'm sorry about your torch. I was looking for you to return it last night when I was bopped on the head and ... well, I was kidnapped.'

Spencer looked as if she were about to say something, then she thought better of it and held her tongue. I continued talking, since I could see that I had Boskin's full attention now.

'You told me the other night that something was going on. Something strange. Well, you were right.'

To my surprise, Boskin threw his onion and knife on to the table, clapped his hands together, and let out a wheezy squeak that may well have been a laugh.

'See! See!' he cackled. 'I told you, didn't I? Old Boskin knows, he does. But no one ever listens. Something's going on around here, sure as the whiskers on my face! Now tell me, policerat ...' and he leant forward eagerly as he spoke, 'what is it?'

I waited a few more seconds, until I was sure he was hanging on my every word.

'I can't tell you, Boskin.'

'What! What do you mean you can't tell me? Fiddlesticks! I'm the caretaker, and if anyone should know what's going on around here, it should be me.'

'Now, listen and listen good. I need your help. There are things afoot —' and here I lowered my voice to a conspiratorial whisper '— things afoot of the gravest danger to Rodent City.'

'I knew it, I knew it, I knew it!' spluttered Boskin. I had him in the palm of my hand now.

'I wish I could tell you more, Boskin, but I don't want to put your life in danger. It's enough for you to know that we have stumbled upon a secret that could destroy us all. I'm sure you understand that it must be pretty important if I, Inspector Octavius O'Malley, am prepared to work alongside a couple of mangy mice.'

'Hey!' yelled Patrick the Magnificent indignantly. 'Who are you calling mangy?'

'Shut up, mouse,' I said.

Boskin looked amused at this, but Spencer just turned her eyes to the roof and sighed loudly enough for everyone to hear.

'Can we just get on with this, please?' she said impatiently.

'Boskin,' I said, 'the only rodents who know about this evil plot, apart from those carrying it out, are the four of us in this room right now. Now, I can't tell you any more about it yet, because to be honest, I'm not sure if I can trust you. In order to win my trust, you have to give me your help. Will you help me, Boskin? Will you help me save Rodent City?'

Boskin's grey whiskers were positively quivering with excitement. I could see that he would sell his own mother to know more about what was going on.

'Of course I'll help. What do you want?' he asked.

'The meetings,' I replied. 'The meetings in the cheese factory. Important people coming and going.'

'You need to know who was there, don't you?' interrupted Boskin.

'No, I know who was there. I need to know when they met. What days, and what times. As many as you can remember.'

'Oh, that's simple,' said Boskin. 'Every fortnight, same day, same time. Wednesday night, six o'clock. Now, let's see, today is Monday, and they didn't meet last Wednesday, so the next one must be the day after tomorrow. Like clockwork, they are.'

'Brilliant!' said Spencer.

'I know I am,' I said, turning around to catch her eye. Now perhaps these mice knew what a great detective I was. I turned back to Boskin. 'So this Wednesday, six o'clock, they'll meet again at the cheese factory.'

'Not quite,' said Boskin. 'Factory's burnt and damaged now, ain't it? Even old Boskin can't clean it up that fast. Specially with you police interrupting me all the time.'

'Hmmm …' I said. 'So where will it be? Have they told you?'

'Not exactly,' wheezed Boskin, 'but old Boskin's no fool. He's worked it out. Mr Remarque himself dropped me a note yesterday. Asked me to go over to a warehouse he owns two blocks from here and give it a special clean-up. Move the boxes off into the corner. Put down some carpet. And bring lots of chairs over, he said. Lots of chairs by Wednesday afternoon at the latest.'

'Boskin,' I said, 'I believe you're absolutely right. Now, tell me, old chap, do you think you can get us into that warehouse so we can spy on the meeting?'

The old caretaker grinned. He reached into his pocket and fished out a huge rusty metal ring. Lots of keys of different shapes and sizes hung from it. They jangled noisily as he shook it in front of his face.

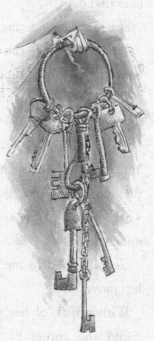

'What do you reckon, Inspector?' he screeched, laughing and shaking the keys at me. 'What do you reckon?'

10
THE GANG

When we left Boskin's rather disreputable little shed I decided to head straight back to my office. I told Spencer I would meet her back at the gang's hideout later that day.

She looked at me carefully.

'I **can** trust you, can't I, O'Malley?' she said. 'You won't do anything stupid like try to arrest us, will you?'

'Don't tempt me, mouse,' I replied. 'Let's get one thing straight right now. I don't like this any more than you do. If I had my way, you'd be in gaol right now. You're nothing better than a common criminal. But for the moment, we've got more important things to worry about. So let's just get through this with a minimum of fuss. Deal?'

'Sounds good to me,' she said. 'Come on, Patrick, let's move.'

With a flick of her tail, Spencer was off, slipping round the corner of the alley with Patrick close behind. I stuck my head around the corner to watch them go, but there was no one there. Tricky.

When I got back to the office there was paperwork all over my desk. There were reports on new crimes, notes from other detectives, and right on top of the pile was a note from Police Chief Carey, saying he needed to see me urgently. This was not good.

Just as I was wondering what to do next, there was a knock on the door and Sergeant Smith stuck his head in.

'Ocko, where have you been? No one's seen you for a couple of days, and the boss is screaming for you.'

'Come in, Sergeant, take a seat,' I said. But even as I did I was thinking to myself: 'Who can I trust? If Carey is in on this plot, who else is in on it too? Surely good

old Sergeant Smith can be trusted. Then again, what if Police Chief Carey is telling him one story, and I'm telling him another? Who will he believe? And even if I **do** tell him what's going on, aren't I just putting him at risk?'

'What is it, Inspector? Are you okay?'

Smith was now sitting opposite me. I realised I had been staring into space, saying nothing, for about a minute.

'I'm fine, Sergeant. But I have something very important to tell you, and I need you to treat it as strictly confidential, okay?'

'Of course,' said Sergeant Smith, sitting up straight in his chair and squaring his shoulders. 'I'm all ears.'

Actually, Sergeant Smith did have very large ears for a rat. They made him look more like a rabbit. But that's not important right now — and anyway, he had them tucked neatly away under his police helmet.

I leant forward and rubbed my paws together.

'For the next few days, I'm going to be working undercover. **Deep** undercover. And no one must know anything about it but you.'

'Jeepers, Ocko, what's this all about?'

'Look, Smith, I can't tell you too much. I don't want to put you in danger. The less you know the better. But I could be about to crack a very big case.'

'Really? A big case? How big?'

'The biggest, Smith, the biggest.'

Sergeant Smith opened his eyes wide and his whiskers began to twitch. He leant forward too and spoke in a hushed voice.

'Is it the River Road Mouse Gang? Is it? I'll bet it's the River Road Mouse Gang. They're the most famous criminal gang in town. Hot dog! Is it, Ocko, is it?'

I paused for a few seconds and pulled on one ear, as if I were trying to make up my mind. Then I sighed.

'Yes, Smith, it is. It's the River Road Mouse Gang. But you must keep that under your hat.' It was a lie, but at least it was fairly close to the truth, and it would explain why I was going to be out of sight for quite some time.

'Hot dog!' said Sergeant Smith again. 'Let me help on this one, Ocko. Let me go undercover too! Please?'

'No, Smith,' I said firmly. 'This is strictly a one-rat operation. I need you here to hold the fort.'

'Oh, but please, Ocko, this is my big chance! I could wear a false set of whiskers and lengthen my tail and pin my ears back and no one would recognise me. I could be your cousin from Rat Valley. I do a really good valley accent, and —'

'Smith!' I snapped. **'Just do as you're told!'**

Smith looked crestfallen.

'That was a curt remark,' he muttered.

'What?' I yelped. 'What did you say about Kurt Remarque? What have you heard?'

Smith looked at me, puzzled. 'I said it was a curt remark. That remark you made was fairly curt.'

'Oh, **curt remark**,' I said with relief. 'I thought you said **Kurt Remarque**.'

'I **did** say curt remark.'

'No, I thought you said Kurt Remarque. You know, **the** Kurt Remarque.'

'Why would I say that? What's **he** got to do with the River Road Mouse Gang?'

'Nothing,' I said quickly, 'nothing at all. Absolutely zero. Forget I said anything, Sergeant. I'm a little confused. I haven't been sleeping well.'

'Is there anything I can do to help?'

'Yes, Smith, there is. Take over my office. Deal with all this paperwork. Keep the other detectives working. Tell Chief Carey I'm on a special assignment and can't be contacted. You don't know where I am, okay? I'm counting on you Smith.'

'No problem, Ocko, you got it.'

I left the office before Sergeant Smith had a chance to ask me any more questions. Curt remark indeed.

****

It took me longer than expected to find the gang's hideout again. I took several wrong turns down blind alleys before I finally wound up outside the anonymous little door.

I lifted my paw to knock, but the door swung open before I had the chance. Patrick the Magnificent was standing there.

'Well, it's about time,' said the annoying little mouse. 'Come on in, we've been holding dinner for you.'

As soon as he spoke, I realised I was starving. When had I last eaten anything? I followed Patrick down a narrow corridor and into what must have been the gang's dining room.

Four mice were seated around a large table, which was covered in plates of food. There were two empty seats.

Spencer sat at the head of the table and she waved me to a seat at the opposite end.

'Ah, at last,' she said. 'Come and join us, Inspector, and let me do the introductions.'

Patrick and Spencer were both wearing the red waistcoat and green trousers they'd had on before, and the other three gang members were dressed the same way. Some sort of uniform, I suspected.

Spencer gestured at three mice sitting at the table with her.

'Meet Larry, Garry and Barry,' she said. 'Larry is the fastest runner you've every seen, Garry climbs like a monkey and Barry is so strong he can lift a human with one hand. Don't worry if you get confused — they're brothers, so they look a little alike. And guys, this is the celebrated Inspector Octavius O'Malley. Ocko to his friends.'

The three brothers grunted in my direction, but said nothing.

'So I presume I've now met the entire River Road Mouse Gang?' I said as I took a seat.

'You have indeed,' said Spencer proudly. 'Surprised?'

'Only that you've got away with things for as long as you have,' I replied. 'You don't look like much to me.'

Barry glared at me (or was it Larry?), and Garry just sneered (or was it Barry?).

'Oh well, let's just say looks can be deceiving,' said Spencer. 'Now, let's eat.'

I turned my attention to the food that covered the table. There were plates of cheese, mounds of crackers and bowls of figs, apricots, cherries and strawberries. There were several kinds of nuts, a big platter of warm sausages, a plate of cold roast chicken and some bowls of what looked like hummus and baba ganoush. (If you don't know what those last two are, just trust me: they're delicious.) There were no doughnuts, but you can't have everything. I tucked in.

For several minutes, we all concentrated on our food, until the silence was broken by Spencer.

'So, Ocko, what did you get up to today?'

'Well, I just went down to the office to put some arrangements in place. Let's just say I won't be missed for a while. We can work in peace.'

'Hmm, I'm impressed. How did you manage that?'

'Easy,' I said, staring hard in her direction. 'I told them I was going undercover to chase the River Road Mouse Gang.'

Larry, Barry and Garry all stopped chewing and looked straight at me, and Patrick the Magnificent almost choked on a large chunk of cheese.

'Don't worry, boys, he's joking,' said Spencer. Then she turned her gaze to me. 'You **are** joking, aren't you, Ocko?'

I noticed she had finally started calling me Ocko.

'No, I'm not joking,' I said. 'It's the perfect cover story. If my Sergeant thinks I'm on your trail, I'll be left alone. And if by chance someone should see me in the company of mice, they'll just think I'm investigating you. After all, you must know the River Road Mouse Gang is the most wanted criminal group in the city.'

'I should hope so,' said Spencer, returning to her food. 'That's always been our aim.'

'Oh, so **that's** been your aim, has it?' I shouted. 'You just want a bit of fame and fortune. You just want to be notorious.' I put down the piece of chicken I had been eating and leant across the table towards her. 'And what about all your victims? Didn't you spare a thought for all of those whose lives were affected by your shocking crimes?'

'What are you talking about, O'Malley?' said Spencer. So I was back to O'Malley now. 'So one of Kurt Remarque's banks lost a bit of money. So the electricity went missing for a couple of hours, and customers at the bakery didn't have their usual choice of bread. Don't you see we're trying to make a point here?'

'No, I don't,' I said stiffly.

'Well, maybe you should open your eyes and look around you, Inspector. Don't you rats always complain about humans? **Monkey people**, you call them. **Picking on the rats**, you moan. Treating you like vermin, blaming you for everything, persecuting you. Well, have you ever stopped for just one minute to think about the way rats treat mice? The way you persecute us, treat us like vermin, blame us for everything?'

'But that's different,' I protested. 'You're ... you're ... mice! You **are** vermin.'

'Oh, **tosh!**' said Spencer, rising to her feet. 'Just listen to yourself! Keep thinking like that and the world will never change. The humans blame the rats, the rats blame the mice. Cats hate dogs, dogs hate cats. Birds think fish are stupid because they can't fly, and fish make fun of birds because they can't swim. What does that mean for flying fish and penguins? Who knows? Who cares? On and on it goes.

'So we're different — who cares? The truth is that we're all more alike than you care to admit. You know what the real problem is, Ocko? The real problem is that we all need someone to pick on. We all need someone to feel superior to. No wonder Kurt Remarque wants to wipe out all the common rats; it's to prove once and for all that he's better than everyone. I'll tell you one thing, Inspector. You have to decide, and decide quickly, whether you're part of the problem or part of the solution.'

Spencer turned tail and began to storm out of the room. I had to think of some reply, something to say quickly.

'Yeah?' I said.

The door slammed behind her, leaving me still at the table with Larry, Garry, Barry and Patrick watching me in an amused sort of way.

'Shut up, mice,' I snapped, before they could say anything.

11

THE MEETING

It was about a quarter to six on Wednesday night and I couldn't see my snout in front of my face. I was hot and sweaty and cramped. This was no condition for a famous Police Inspector to be in. To make matters even worse, Patrick the Magnificent was sitting on my lap and Spencer was squashed up beside me in the darkness.

'Is that your tail?' It was Spencer talking, as she fidgeted around in the confined space to try and get comfortable.

'No, I don't think so,' I said.

Spencer fidgeted around again, and suddenly I felt a sharp pain.

'**That's** my tail!' I said quickly. 'Now, could you stop sitting on it please?'

'Sorry,' said Spencer, moving a bit further round. 'How's that?'

'Better,' I said. 'But I think it might be a good idea if we all kept quiet, don't you? And I mean all of us.'

'Sure,' said Spencer.

'Sure,' said another voice from the darkness, which must have come from Garry. Or Larry. Or Barry.

Have you guessed where we all were yet?

We were inside Kurt Remarque's second factory, the one that Boskin had spent all day cleaning and preparing for the meeting.

True to his word, he had pushed all the old boxes off into one corner to make room for about a dozen chairs to be set up.

One of those boxes, however, had a small hole in it. A hole just big enough for a rat, or perhaps a mouse, to peek through.

I was inside that box, crowded in with the River Road Mouse Gang, waiting for Kurt Remarque's meeting to begin.

As the room slowly started to fill up, I saw Mayor Mottley, fat and sleek, take a seat at the very front of the room. Police Chief Carey was just behind him, and I noticed that his assistant, Deputy Chief Jenkins, was there too. 'How many other police are involved?' I thought to myself.

After that, Spencer had **her** turn looking through the eyehole, and she whispered a few other names to me.

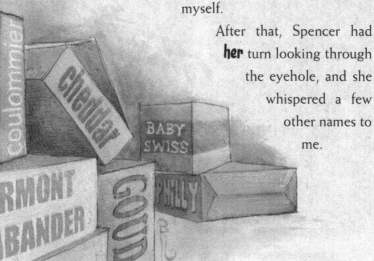

'There's Crumbley, the baker,' she hissed, 'and Patterson, who runs that chain of jewellery stores. Oh, and Vellum, the head of the electricity company. Gosh, Ocko, anyone who's anyone is here … Uh-oh, look at this!'

She stepped back and I took her place at the eyehole.

There, amid all the well-known rats, two strangers were walking slowly into the room. Very big strangers. Humans, in fact. One was sneaky-looking, short and thin, although he was still large enough to tower over all the rats. The other was huge — tall and fat and almost completely bald. They sat down at the back of the room and stared around suspiciously at the rats.

Most of the rats were chatting quietly in small groups, but suddenly everyone fell silent. A door at one end of the room had opened, and Kurt Remarque marched to the head of the room, where a lectern stood facing all the chairs. He cleared his throat loudly. The meeting had begun.

Spencer and I took turns watching silently through the hole, while the other members of the gang listened as best as they could. Between the six of us, we caught most of what went on during the meeting. This is what happened:

Kurt Remarque called everyone to order, and began to speak.

'Since our last meeting, gentlerats,' he said, 'much has taken place. I told you then that the key to our success would be enlisting humans to present our plan to the Council, where it is bound to succeed. Well, I'm happy to say that we have found the ideal candidates. Can I introduce you all to the Borrow brothers?'

At this point, the two men sitting at the back of the room got to their feet, looking a little self-conscious. The small, sneaky-looking one glanced around craftily, as if he were sizing up the enemy. The big fat one just looked happy, smiling rather stupidly at everyone.

Kurt Remarque continued. 'Gentlerats, allow me to introduce you to the Borrow brothers. Gonzaga' (and at the mention of his name, the smaller of the two nodded ever so slightly) 'and Septimus' (and here the tall, fat one waved) 'Borrow, to be precise. The Borrow brothers have been in the cleaning and pest control business for almost thirty years, and they have recently arrived in the city from a neighbouring county. Gentlemen, perhaps you could tell us a bit about yourselves?'

Gonzaga Borrow looked as if he would rather say nothing at all, but straight away the bigger brother began talking.

'We're cleaners, we do all sorts of cleaning, and we do pest control as well. We've got a nice van, and lots

of cool equipment. We got chased out of the last city we were in, cos we got in trouble, but —'

'Shut up, brother!' hissed the smaller one. 'You talk too much.'

Septimus, the bigger brother, looked hurt. He sat down grumpily in his chair, pulled a large doughnut out of his pocket and began to eat it.

Stuck inside the dark, cramped box, I immediately began to feel a little hungry myself. **Mmm, doughnuts!**

Having managed to stop his brother from talking, Gonzaga decided to pick up the story himself.

'Yes, well, it's true we have recently relocated to this fair city of yours after running our company for many successful years, ah … somewhere else. For that reason, we are keen to drum up as much new business as we can, and this rat extermination plan of yours sounds most interesting.'

Police Chief Carey jumped to his feet. 'I am interested to learn why you are prepared to work with rats. Most humans hate us.'

'Yes,' added Mayor Mottley. 'What **do** you think of rats?'

'I hate rats!' said Septimus between mouthfuls of doughnut.

'What?' said Kurt Remarque.

'Well, what he means,' added Gonzaga quickly, squinting around the room, 'is that he hates **most** rats. Present company excepted, of course.'

'No, I hate **all** rats,' said Septimus. 'Ouch! What did you kick me for?'

'You must forgive my brother,' said Gonzaga through gritted teeth. 'His mouth works faster than his brain. In fact, I'm not sure that his brain works at all. He's as stupid as an ox, but luckily he's as strong as an ox, too. He can carry two barrels of poison on each shoulder, so believe me, we'll need him.' Gonzaga looked at his large brother, who was sitting there munching placidly on his doughnut. 'Septimus, why don't you just leave the talking to me? You just finish your doughnut.'

'Sure brother, sure.'

'Gentlemen,' said Gonzaga, spreading his arms out wide as he addressed all the rats in the room, 'what my brother means to say is that we hate **ordinary** rats, not the **extraordinary** rats that I see before me in this room. We hate common rats, we hate mice, we hate cockroaches and fleas and dust mites and dust as well. We are cleaners and pest controllers, or as I like to say, exterminators. But let me confide something to you.'

Gonzaga left his seat, walked to the front of the room, and stood next to Kurt Remarque.

'I can see you are all men of the world — um, excuse me, **rats** of the world. You understand the way things work, so let me speak frankly. If there is one thing I love more than exterminating things, it is making a lot of money. Ten million dollars. **TEN MILLION DOLLARS!** Half for you, and half for us. With your map telling us where the rats are, and our expertise in efficient extermination, there's no stopping us.'

Gonzaga's eyes were glinting with greed as he stood in front of the room of rats, rubbing his hands together.

'But what happens when it's all over?' asked a voice from the middle of the room. It was Crumbley the baker. 'What happens when the rats here in this room return to the city to rebuild our empire? The human Mayor will know he's been tricked, and you'll be arrested.'

'Ah, but that's the perfect part of it,' boomed Kurt Remarque. 'Tell them, Mr Borrow.'

'I hate rats,' came a muffled, doughnut voice from the back.

'Not **you**, Mr Borrow,' said Kurt to Septimus, 'the **other** Mr Borrow.'

'Well, you see,' said Gonzaga, 'they can't arrest what they can't catch. As soon as this gig is over and they pay us the money, we'll be out of here faster than you can say "Cheese". You won't catch us hanging around here to face the music.'

'But you'll lose your business,' said Crumbley. 'Everything you've worked to build up over the years.'

'Well, listen,' said Gonzaga conspiratorially, 'that's not much of a problem. You see, as my brother kinda mentioned before, we left our last town under a bit of a cloud, so to speak. Not everyone was totally happy with our cleaning methods, I guess you could say. So if we have to blow this town too, well, we have a bit of experience at doing that. Besides, with ten million bucks in our pockets, we can go wherever we like and do whatever we like.'

'You mean five million,' said Kurt Remarque.

'Oh yeah, sure, five million,' said Gonzaga. 'Our share.'

I sat there in the cardboard box, listening to all of this, and made up my mind about a few things. Number one, the Borrow brothers were crooks. After ten years as a Police Inspector, you get a nose for these sorts of things, and I knew a crook when I heard one. Number two, the Borrow brothers were planning to take off with **all** the money, not just their share. And number three, they didn't care how many rats died after they'd carried out their devious plan. Number four, I **really** felt like a doughnut.

The meeting ended with all the rats there voting to work with the Borrow brothers, and to hand over to them the map of Rodent City.

Kurt Remarque clapped his paws together loudly twice, and an assistant entered the room carrying a small black box. Kurt opened the lid and pulled out a little leather-bound book.

THE MAP!

He walked over to Gonzaga Borrow, the smaller and smarter of the two brothers. With his left paw, he passed over the map. With his right, he shook hands with Gonzaga.

'Congratulations Mr Borrow,' he said, 'you're about to make yourselves — and us — very rich indeed.'

Gonzaga smiled nastily and tried to remove his hand. It looked as if he'd never shaken hands with a rat before and wasn't particularly enjoying the experience.

But Kurt Remarque wouldn't let go. He kept a firm grip on Gonzaga's sweaty hand, and looked into his eyes.

'Just make sure this plan works,' he said emphatically, and finally released Gonzaga's hand.

After that, the meeting was over.

I waited for several minutes after the last rat had left the room before I carefully pushed open the top of the box and crawled out. Spencer and the rest of the gang followed me, and we were soon sitting together in the empty chairs.

'Well, Ocko,' said Spencer, 'this is definitely serious. I thought when they found out the book of minutes was missing after the explosion, they might back off. But it looks like they're really going through with it.'

'It looks like it, it certainly does.'

'So what do we do now?' put in Patrick the Magnificent.

For once, I didn't tell him to shut up. Either I was getting used to this little mouse, or I was just too tired and depressed after being cooped up in that cardboard box for so long, listening to such evil plans.

'Well, Patrick,' I replied, 'the first thing is we tell no one about what we've heard here today. I need time to think it all through properly before our next move. And until then, no one must know but us. **No one —** you understand?'

Just then I heard a **BUMP** from the back of the room. I looked over nervously to where the boxes were all stacked up and something caught my eye.

It caught Spencer's eye too.

'That box over there,' she whispered, 'it's ... it's moving.'

Sure enough, the box right next to the one we had been in was wobbling slightly. Right before our astonished eyes, it began to rock back and forth, until finally it fell onto its side with a dull **THUD**.

The top flap of the box flew open and out crawled the crumpled, hunched-over figure of ...

Boskin.

'Oh, my aching back!' groaned the old caretaker as he got unsteadily to his feet. 'It was hell in there.'

'Boskin!' I yelled. 'What were you doing in there? I thought I told you to let us in, organise a hiding place, and then get out of here!'

'So what?' screeched the old rat. 'Did you think I was going to let you have all the fun? He began to shuffle in our direction. 'So, this all sounds pretty serious. What are you going to do now, Inspector?'

What indeed? All the town's rats, and mice as well for that matter, were threatened with destruction.

I was the only one who could save the day, and all I had to help me were a bunch of criminal mice and a broken-down old caretaker.

'Someone get me a doughnut,' I moaned. **I'm starving!**

12
OCKO FIGHTS BACK

Have I mentioned what a great detective I am? What a rat among rats? Other, lesser rodents would have given up when faced with the odds confronting me. But not me — not Ocko.

You see, the thing to do when you're facing a huge and complicated problem is to get organised.

I decided to get organised.

Like it or not, I was stuck with five mice and a grumpy old rat as my associates, the only ones I could trust. And right now, what we needed most was a base, somewhere we could all work and stay together. Even though I trusted those mice, I was determined not to let them out of my sight if I could help it. A wise old rat once said, 'Keep your friends close, and your enemies closer.' All I knew was that, friends or enemies, we were all going to be **very** close for a while.

I couldn't go back to my office and I didn't want to stay with Spencer and her gang in their hideout. Even though we were working together, it still felt like

enemy territory. Boskin's shed, apart from being filthy, was too dangerous — what if Kurt Remarque sent someone round with more instructions?

'Think, Ocko, think.' Suddenly it came to me: **the old schoolhouse**. Perfect!

I told Boskin to grab what he needed and meet me over there and then I told Spencer to do the same and bring her gang as well. There was a bit of huffing and puffing on the part of Boskin once he realised that he would be living with mice, but I was insistent.

'Now listen, Boskin,' I said. 'No one asked you to hide in that box and get involved in all of this, but now you **are** involved and that's all there is to it. Mice or no mice, I'm not letting you out of my sight, so you'd better just get used to it.'

The River Road Mouse Gang were far less trouble. Given how Spencer kept going on about being persecuted by rats, I expected her to put up more of a fight, but she surprised me by agreeing straight away. I realised the gang just loved a bit of adventure more than anything else.

So now here we all were, gathered around a big table in the main hall of the old schoolhouse. The school hadn't been used for over a year, since one of my police detectives discovered it was being used as a storage area for stolen goods. One of the teacher rats turned out to be the main culprit and was duly arrested. The goods were confiscated, the school was moved to a new location right next to the church, and the buildings had lain abandoned since then. The Police Department officially owned them now, but I knew for a fact that no one ever went near them, which made them perfect for us. Boskin knocked up a few rough beds in one of the classrooms, the toilet block still worked, and the tuck shop would serve just fine as our kitchen.

We had our campaign headquarters. We were set. It was time to show these guys what Inspector Octavius O'Malley was made of.

I stood up grandly from my chair, ready to make my big speech. Unfortunately, I managed to hook the end of my tail around the leg of the chair, and as I stepped back the chair fell over, knocking down the easel I had carefully set up behind it. The easel was loaded with large sheets of white paper, Textas, pencils, a long pointer and a large roll of black tape. It all fell to the floor around my feet.

Patrick the Magnificent burst out laughing. Spencer contented herself with simply crossing her arms and smiling, as if she'd seen it all before. Boskin, however, leapt to his feet. He shuffled over, bent down and began collecting things from the floor, grumbling to himself the whole way through.

'More mess, more mess, more for Boskin to clean up! It never ends, never ends!'

I joined in (the cleaning up, that is, not the grumbling) and when everything was back in place I started my speech again.

'Now, I've been doing a lot of thinking, and I can't see too many ways out of our predicament. It's a real stinker. We have to approach this the way I'd normally handle a police investigation: calmly and logically. So, what do we know?'

'We know we're all doomed,' said Larry, the fast-running member of the River Road Gang. 'Kurt Remarque has got every angle covered, and every powerful rat on his side. There's no hope, and I'm too bored to sit around listening to all this theorising.'

He jumped up and disappeared out the door.

'Where's he off to?' I asked.

'Who knows?' answered Spencer. 'Don't worry, he won't go far. He's always a bit pessimistic, is old Larry. Fast, but pessimistic. So where were we up to?'

'We were up to the bit where we've got no hope,' put in Patrick the Magnificent.

'**No, no, no!**' I said in exasperation. 'We were up to the bit where I was asking if anyone had any ideas.'

'Well, you're the Police Inspector,' said Garry. (Or maybe it was Barry. He looked pretty strong, so I guess it **must** have been Barry.) 'Why don't you just arrest everyone?'

'Yeah,' said Patrick. 'After all, that book we found had all the evidence you need.'

'That book you found?' I said. 'Don't you mean that book you **stole?**'

'Whatever,' said Patrick.

'Anyway,' I went on, 'there's a big problem with arresting everybody. There's no way I could arrest people like Kurt Remarque and Mayor Mottley without special permission from Police Chief Carey. And as we all know, he's not very likely to give me permission, is he?'

'He's more likely to throw you in gaol,' said Spencer.

'Exactly,' I agreed.

'So what next?' she said to no one in particular.

'We just have to foil their plan,' said Patrick.

'But how?' Spencer shot back. 'They've got THE MAP, they've got the Borrow brothers, and they've got the Chief of Police and the Mayor on their side.'

'Very true,' I concurred.

'Well, what's your big idea then?' asked Patrick in annoyance.

'I don't have one, mouse,' I said. 'But I'll tell you one very important thing that ten years of experience have taught me. Good police work is made up of lots of **little** ideas rather than one **BIG** idea. You break open a case by working away in many different areas at once.'

'So what does that mean?' said Patrick.

'That means we need information, while we've still got time to get it. We've got to check out these Borrow brothers and see what their plans are. We need to know what sort of poison they'll be using, where they'll get it. We need to know if they're really going to win the competition.'

I began to pace back and forth, which I did a lot of when I was thinking. I also tripped over the easel again, which I also seemed to do a lot of when I was thinking. This time, no one bothered to pick it up.

'We also need someone to stake out Kurt Remarque's office and follow both him and his assistant wherever they go. That's a two-rat — oh, sorry, a two-**rodent** — operation. Barry, Garry, are you up for that?'

Barry and Garry both looked at Spencer. She nodded.

'Sure,' they said together.

'Okay. Now, Patrick. Why don't you put that chewing gum and toothpick to good use and break into Mayor Mottley's office tonight?'

'No problems,' said Patrick. 'What am I looking for?'

'I don't know,' I said. 'Let's just see if there's anything interesting there — papers, plans, anything at all.'

'What about me?' squawked Boskin. 'What about old Boskin?'

'For now, I want you to stay here at headquarters,' I said. 'Someone has to hold the fort. Maybe you could cook us some dinner later.'

'How glamorous,' muttered Boskin.Right at that moment the door burst open and Larry raced in, obviously out of breath. He was balancing a huge newspaper on his head.

'Look at this!' he gasped, holding out the paper to me. It was opened at an article on page 5.

I scanned it quickly.

RAT CONTRACT AWARDED

The Municipal Council announced today that the contract to exterminate all the city's rats has been awarded to a consortium led by Borrow Brothers Cleaning and Pest Control, 54 Squash Street, Bugville.

The process will be carried out in precisely four days' time.

All citizens are advised to stay in their houses next Sunday between 4 and 5 am while poison flooding is in progress.

'Well,' I said, 'we don't have much time. Spencer, I think you and I need to pay a visit to these Borrow brothers as soon as possible.'

'I'm with you, Ocko,' she said. 'Let's do it.'

13
WITH THE BORROW BROTHERS

We left after lunch, Spencer and I. Boskin had made a batch of lemon pancakes that were simply irresistible, so I ate six of them. Well, okay, it was actually eight, but you have to remember that pancakes are excellent brain food. Almost as good as doughnuts.

We travelled carefully and discreetly, because we were moving through the human side of town. That's always a tricky business. You monkey people can be particularly nasty when you come across rodents. You fight like cornered rats.

After a quick trip along the Main Gutter Line as far as the post office, we crossed over to a stormwater drain, slipped down it and headed underground. Spencer led the way — until something rather unfortunate happened.

She had just disappeared around a corner and I was about twenty metres behind her. I had slowed down to adjust my jacket, which suddenly seemed a little tight and uncomfortable. Perhaps it was all the pancakes.

Just as I stopped to loosen a button, it popped off and flew through the air. I was about to chase it when I heard a commotion up ahead. I went to investigate.

Spencer was standing in the middle of the path surrounded by six rats. They looked like trouble.

'Well, waddya know,' one of them was saying. 'Looks like this little mousie has lost her way.'

'Yeah, sweetie,' said another. 'Don't you know this is rat territory down here?'

'I should've guessed from the smell,' said Spencer. Boy, I thought, that was telling them.

Just then one of the rats noticed me.

'What do **you** want?' he said gruffly. 'Get out of here if you don't want trouble.'

'Oh, trouble is precisely what I **do** want,' I replied, stepping forward. 'Inspector O'Malley is the name, and considering the way you lot behave, I'm surprised we haven't run into each other before. Now, clear off before I have you all arrested.'

'Yeah, you and what army?' said one of them.

'How come you're hanging round with a mouse anyway?' said another. 'That's got to be against some kind of law.'

'Okay, that's it,' I said. 'You've had your warning.'

I stepped up to the nearest rat and grabbed him in the officially registered Police Arm Lock Number 203. Check it, it's in the manual. He yelped in surprise as I slipped one of his arms into my regulation police handcuffs. As one of his mates rushed up to help, I grabbed him as well, forcing his arm behind his back and clicking the second handcuff shut around his wrist.

The two rats were now handcuffed together, and before they knew what I was doing I had pushed them up against the wall and padlocked the handcuffs to one of the pipes that ran all along the walls of the sewer.

That took care of those two, but there were four more, and they all came towards me at once. It was the wrong time for me to realise that the loose buttonhole on my jacket had somehow become tangled up in the handcuffs. I was trapped, with four ugly rat hoodlums bearing down on me fast.

It all happened so quickly I almost missed it. Two of the rats heading my way fell forward on their faces. For a moment I thought they'd tripped — until I saw Spencer flying through the air. She kicked out with one leg, catching the third rat right on the end of his snout, while with one hand she karate-chopped the fourth rat in the stomach.

Well, that was enough for the troublemakers. They all turned tail and ran, except for the two in the handcuffs, who sat there looking glum as I disentangled myself and went over to Spencer.

'Thanks,' I said. 'That was pretty impressive.'

'For a mouse?' said Spencer.

'No, for anyone.'

'Well, you're no slouch either, Ocko. What'll we do about these two?'

Spencer pointed at the handcuffed rats, sitting together on the floor of the sewer.

I pulled the padlock key from my pocket, strode over and put it on the ground just out of reach of the two captors.

'Let that be a lesson to you,' I said. 'When someone finally comes along to release you, I want you to return those handcuffs in perfect condition to the Central Police Station and ask for Inspector O'Malley. I'll deal with you then; right now I'm too busy.'

'Do you really think they'll do that?' whispered Spencer after I walked back to her.

'Of course not,' I replied, 'but what do you want to do — take them along with us? Besides, I can always get new cuffs. Now, where were we?'

****

Half an hour later, Spencer and I were standing outside an old broken-down warehouse. It stood at the end of Squash Street, a narrow, dark alleyway, its paint peeling and its elderly weatherboards showing obvious signs of rot. Outside the building was a large black van, and printed on the side of the van was:

Borrow Brothers

Cleaning Services · Pest Extermination · Rubbish Removal

Serving the Community since 1972

We skirted round the van until we found the back entrance to the Borrow Brothers warehouse.

'I hope this lock isn't too complicated,' said Spencer. 'We'll be in trouble without Patrick the Magnificent here to help us.'

'Oh, I'm sure there's nothing he can do that I can't do,' I said, striding up to the door. 'Hmm, a Yale double lock. That's a tough one. I'll bet even that little mouse would have trouble with this.'

'I'm not so sure,' said Spencer, 'but there is one thing that Patrick always says. Never ignore the obvious.

Have you tried turning the handle? It might be unlocked.'

'Oh, don't be silly,' I said. 'As if they'd keep it unlocked!'

I turned the handle. It was unlocked.

Spencer looked as if she were about to say something, but I put a finger to my lips to silence her. We slipped through the door and down a long corridor.

I heard voices coming faintly from the distance. At the end of the corridor on the right was a door, and as we drew near the voices grew louder, but I couldn't make out what they were saying.

'We've got to get in there,' I whispered. 'But it's too dangerous to open the door. They might see us.'

'Look,' said Spencer quietly. She pointed up above the door, where there was a small window shaped like a half-circle opened slightly to let the air in. 'We have to get up there. But how?'

'Rope. We have to find some rope.'

We retraced our steps. About halfway back along the corridor was another door, this time on the left. There were no voices coming from behind this one, so I opened it and cautiously poked my head inside. It was a huge storage room, packed with all sorts of junk. It didn't take long to find a jumble of ropes in one corner. All different sizes they were, tangled up in an unholy mess. That sort of chaos really gets me mad — but this was no time for complaining.

Spencer pounced eagerly on the pile and soon found just what she was after: a long piece of thin, strong-looking nylon rope. She tied a loop in one end and coiled it loosely over her shoulder.

Back at the far end of the corridor, Spencer pointed out the little latch on the bottom of the half-opened window. She threw the looped end of the rope nimbly into the air and just missed the latch. She threw again and missed by even more.

'Let me try,' I whispered.

I threw the rope and the loop caught on the catch first time. No one was more surprised than I.

Spencer pulled the loop tight and scampered up the rope, settling herself on a narrow shelf just above the door. I followed, and squashed in beside her. I was much bigger, of course, so I had to keep hold of the rope to stop myself from slipping down.

I looked through the window. The Borrow brothers were sitting side by side at a small table. Over the massive shoulder of the big one, Septimus, I could see the map book open at a plan of the whole of Rodent City.

As I watched, Septimus dropped his huge hand onto the centre of the book like a slab of meat.

'There's a lot of places to poison,' he said.

'Don't you worry about that, I've got it all worked out,' returned Gonzaga, the smaller one. 'You see this?'

He pulled out a sheet of paper that was under the map book and unfolded it.

'Looks like spaghetti,' said Septimus. 'That reminds me, I'm hungry. Do we have any spaghetti?'

'You're always hungry, you great oaf. Now, pay attention.'

Gonzaga started pointing at different sections of the sheet in front of him. I craned my neck as far as I could, but I couldn't quite see what was on the sheet. I glanced over at Spencer to find out if she could see anything, but she just shrugged.

'I've checked all our storerooms,' continued Gonzaga, 'and we've got about three dozen hoses of different lengths and sizes. Now, if we couple them together using standard attachments and join everything to a common feeder tube —'

'It looks just like spaghetti!' repeated Septimus.

I could hear Gonzaga gritting his teeth, even from where I was perched above the door.

'I **know** it looks like spaghetti, but could we just focus on the problem at hand for a moment?' he snapped. 'This "spaghetti" is going to distribute rat poison from one central spot to all over town, into every rat hole, cellar and sewer in the city.'

'Will it really go that far?' asked Septimus, who seemed to have forgotten about spaghetti for a moment.

'Well, it'll point everything in the right direction, anyway. Gravity, water pressure and the map will do the rest.'

'And it all comes from one central spot?' asked Septimus, again plonking his fat sausage of a finger down in the middle of the page.

'That's right,' said Gonzaga. 'I'll be setting up my own patented poison pumping station right here.'

He jabbed the piece of paper.

'Where?' I thought. **'Where?'** I couldn't see a thing.

At that moment, Gonzaga refolded the paper and slipped it into the back pocket of his dusty grey trousers. **Darn!**

'That just leaves one thing, big brother,' said Gonzaga.

'What? Lunch? How about spaghetti?'

'No, not lunch,' said Gonzaga. 'The poison. We're not going to get far without poison, are we?'

'Oh, yes, poison,' said Septimus.

'Now, are you sure your supplier can deliver?'

'Of course, little brother. Top-quality rat poison, and I got a really good price, too.'

'A good price?' asked Gonzaga suspiciously.

'The best,' said Septimus. 'I drove a hard bargain.'

'You? Drove a hard bargain? You couldn't drive a hard bargain if it was parked right in front of you with all the doors open and the engine running! You have all the negotiating skills of a door post!'

'Don't worry, little brother,' said Septimus, looking a little injured. 'Four hundred drums of top-quality rat poison at rock-bottom prices.' He rubbed his hands together. 'Now, let's eat. I suggest spaghetti.'

The two brothers got up from the table, collected up their maps and papers, and headed for the door we were hiding above. Spencer and I just had time to scamper down the rope and hide in the shadows as the door opened.

Septimus barrelled out first, followed by Gonzaga. The rope we'd used to climb up was still hanging there, and it flicked Gonzaga in the face.

'What's **this** doing here?' he yelled.

'Beats me,' said Septimus. 'Looks a bit like a piece of spaghetti, though, doesn't it?'

'Just clean it up,' said Gonzaga wearily. 'There's always so much mess around here!'

Septimus reached up and grabbed the end of the rope. The slightest of tugs from his massive arm, and it broke clean away from the latch, coming down with a loud **SNAP** like the cracking of a whip. Beside me in the darkness, Spencer shivered.

The two brothers walked down the corridor, still arguing. They passed within centimetres of us.

'Let's get out of here,' I said to Spencer under my breath. She nodded eagerly.

We left the same way we'd come in, as quickly and quietly as we could.

14
KURT AND THE MAYOR

'More coffee?'

I nodded, and Spencer topped up my cup. We were sitting round a table in the old schoolhouse. Boskin had prepared a perfectly serviceable dinner of beans on toast, and the room was spick-and-span. The old caretaker had been hard at work while the rest of the gang had been out on their investigations.

I had already told everyone about what we'd overheard at the Borrow brothers', and now it was Patrick's turn to report in.

He had hardly been able to contain himself while Spencer and I described our adventure, and now he burst out excitedly.

'It was brilliant!' he exploded, leaning over the table and spilling most of his coffee. I could hear Boskin grumbling in the background.

'Let **me** start,' said Barry, the strongest member of the River Road Mouse Gang. 'After all, it began at Kurt Remarque's place, didn't it?'

'Okay,' said Patrick reluctantly, 'but don't string it out.'

Barry glared at him, then began his story.

'Well, I went over to Kurt's place, just like you asked.'

'We both did!' put in Garry, who you probably remember was the one who could climb like a monkey.

'Yeah,' went on Barry, 'and we had to fight our way past this huge ginger cat who almost killed us.'

'I know that cat,' I said coolly. 'It's not so tough.'

'Maybe not for a rat,' replied Barry indignantly, 'but I bet I'm the only mouse in Rodent City strong enough to handle it. It swiped Garry here with one of its paws and he finished up halfway across the alley behind a rubbish bin.'

'You were incredible,' said Garry, rubbing the back of his neck as he remembered the attack.

'Yes, I was,' said Barry proudly. 'As soon as Garry went flying, I really gave that cat a piece of my mind. **POW! WHACK!** I don't think we'll be seeing him for a while.'

'Yes, I'm sure you were magnificent,' I put in a little impatiently, 'but can we get to the point?'

'That **is** the point,' said Barry. 'You see, after I taught that cat a lesson, I ran over to the bin to see how Garry was, and right at that moment Kurt Remarque's door flew open. I just had time to duck down behind the bin and make sure Garry didn't make any noise.'

'No problems there,' said Garry. 'After all, I was unconscious at the time.'

'Yeah, he was. Well, anyway, this shadowy figure in a big coat and a big hat came out the door and scurried up the alleyway.'

'Who was it?' I said.

'Well, it was really hard to tell because of the big coat and the tall hat, but just as he swept past us the coat flew up a little at the back and I saw a flash of fur. Pure white, it was.'

'Kurt Remarque,'
I breathed.

'None other,' said Barry.

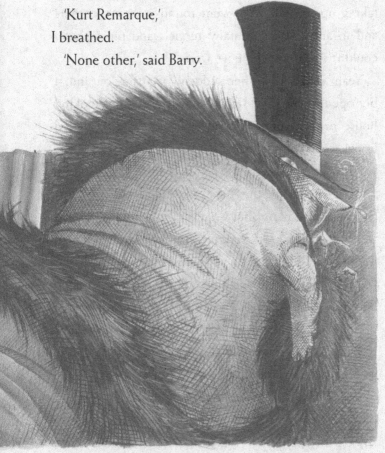

'So what did you do?'

'Well, I woke up Garry,' said Barry.

'You kicked me!' said Garry, a little indignantly.

'Whatever,' said Barry, who was determined not to be distracted from his story. 'I woke you up, didn't I, and we followed him. We kept our distance; he never knew we were there.'

'We must have walked for kilometres,' said Garry, taking up the tale. 'We went round so many corners and in and out of so many tunnels and pipes that I couldn't work out where we were.'

'Yeah,' said Barry. 'Then suddenly we came out into a big open square, and I could see a really cool-looking house in front of us. About four storeys tall, all red brick with shiny steel doors and bars on all the windows.'

'That sounds like the Mayor's house,' I said.

'It was,' said Barry, 'but we didn't know that then, did we? Anyway, Kurt Remarque marched straight up to the big steel front door and banged on it real loud.'

'Yeah,' said Garry, 'and we couldn't get close enough because there was nowhere to hide, so we saw a doorway in the building closest to us, and we went to hide over there until we could work out what to do ...'

'And they ran straight into **me!**' put in Patrick.

'**You?** What were **you** doing there?' I asked.

'Don't you remember?' said Patrick. 'You sent me to spy on the Mayor. He wasn't in his office, so I went to his house, and I was hanging around in the doorway trying to work out what my next step should be when these guys showed up.'

'Yeah,' said Barry. 'We all watched Kurt walk into the Mayor's house, and as soon as he went inside two rats came out and stood in front of the door like they were guarding it. So we didn't know what to do.'

'I knew what to do!' said Patrick proudly. 'I remembered hearing once that the Mayor has a private office on the fourth floor of his house, and I figured that's where he and Kurt would go to talk. So I led Barry and Garry down a side alley to the back entrance.'

'And there were guards there, too,' said Garry.

'Yeah, big ugly rats,' said Patrick. Then he glanced in my direction. 'No offence,' he added.

'None taken,' I said through gritted teeth. 'But can we get to the point?'

'We're getting there,' said Patrick, 'but first I have to explain how brilliant we were. So anyway, we couldn't get in the front or the back, so we went back around to the side, only we couldn't get to the house because there was this huge brick wall between the alley and the house with barbed wire all over the top.'

'So what did you do?' rasped Boskin. He had joined us at the table after cleaning up the spilt coffee, and was obviously fascinated by Patrick's tale of adventure.

However, it was Barry who spoke next.

'I punched a hole right in the wall!' he said proudly.

'You should have seen it,' said Garry. 'One punch, and **WHAM!**'

'Strongest mouse in the universe,' said Barry proudly. 'No one can beat me.'

Patrick picked up the story.

'So anyway, now we were right next to the side wall of the house, and it was Garry's turn.'

'Of course!' I said. I was getting excited now too, in spite of myself. 'He climbs like a monkey, doesn't he?'

'Like a regular chimpanzee,' said Patrick.

'Like an orang-utan!' said Garry proudly.

'So I climbed onto Garry's back,' said Patrick, 'and up we went. Straight up the side of the house as if we had a ladder. All the way to the fourth floor, where there was a side window.'

'Which was locked,' added Garry.

'But that was no match for me,' said Patrick. 'I had that baby open in two seconds flat, and we were inside! The window opened into a sort of hallway at the top of the staircase. At the end of the hall was the door to the Mayor's private office ...'

'... and it was wide open!' said Garry. 'Can you believe that? All that security, and then they sit in an office with the door wide open, plain as day.'

'So we heard everything,' said Patrick.

'Finally!' I said. 'We get to the point. So what did you hear?'

'Central Station. Sunday at 6.05am.'

'What about it?' I said. 'What does that mean?'

'That's the first train out of town on Sunday morning. As it happens, it's heading for the coast, taking all those humans out of town for a day at the seaside, but that's not important right now.'

'Well for goodness' sake, will you tell something that **is** important?' I turned to Spencer in frustration. 'Tell me, do all mice take this long to tell a story, or is it just something your gang specialises in?'

'Patrick, you'd better get to the point,' said Spencer. 'I think our Police Inspector is running out of patience.'

'I'm running out of life!' I said. 'I'll die of old age if something doesn't happen soon.'

'**The point is,**' said Patrick with exaggerated politeness, 'that Kurt Remarque and the Mayor and all the other plotters will be on that train. While the Borrow brothers are flooding every rat hole, street and alleyway with deadly poison, Kurt and his mob will be comfortably settled in a storage bin under the restaurant car of the 6.05am train to the coast.'

'**Aha!**' I said.

'And that's not all,' added Garry. 'The Mayor is arranging for all the public money held in Rodent City's accounts to be drawn out and made into a single bank cheque. That cheque will be made payable to CASH, and they're going to take it with them on the train.'

'But that must be millions of dollars!' said Spencer. She sounded outraged. 'Millions of dollars in public money — money that's meant for schools and hospitals and all sorts of things!'

'Yeah, well, they're taking it all,' said Patrick, 'although I'm not sure if it's as much as you think. The Mayor told Kurt Remarque he thought there was probably only a few hundred thousand in ready cash. Kurt didn't sound too happy.'

'Yeah,' said Garry. 'Remember what he said? He shouted, **If I ran my businesses the way you run this city, Mottley, I wouldn't last five minutes!**'

'That's right,' said Patrick, 'I remember now. Kurt Remarque said he had millions in his own accounts. Anyway, that's about it. Kurt, the Mayor, the Police Chief and all the others will be heading out of town on Sunday morning with all the public money they can get their hands on, and the rest of us will be left to face the poison.'

'Not if **I** can stop them!' I said boldly.

But even as I spoke, I was thinking to myself: 'Yes, Ocko, that's all well and good. But **can** you stop them? **Can** you?'

15
FIRE
AND
RAIN

The Borrow brothers were right there, in the centre of the town's main square. They were surrounded by hundreds of barrels filled with deadly poison. The barrels were stacked on top of each other, reaching up into the sky like the columns of a vast Tower of Pisa.

The square was filled with rats. Thousands of them. Old rats, young rats, families with kids. Why wasn't anyone doing anything? The Borrow brothers were right there, connecting huge hoses up to the barrels. Why didn't somebody stop them? The rats were all smiling and laughing, setting up picnics, playing games. Of course. I was the one. I had to stop them.

But something was wrong. I was running into the square as fast as I could, and I didn't seem to be getting any closer. No matter how fast I ran, the square was still too far away. I kept turning corners and dodging around buildings and running across cobblestones, but it made no difference. I could see everything perfectly, but I was no closer than I'd been at the start.

And now the hoses were connected. Both Borrow brothers had a hose in their hands, and they were pointing them up into the sky, bracing themselves and leaning back with their legs wide apart,

and now the poison was spraying up into the sky, huge jets of deadly red liquid that came down like rain on the crowds of rats in the square.

I was running and running and the poison was spraying and spraying and all the rats were laughing and smiling, and everyone was dancing around in the square as the deadly poison rained down …

I sat upright in bed, suddenly wide awake. It took me a few seconds to shake off my dream and realise that I was still being rained on. I was in my camp bed in one of the classrooms of the old schoolhouse, and it was raining on me. What was going on?

I could hear yelling and the crash of falling objects. It sounded like pots and pans, and the shrill yelling sounded like Boskin.

I leapt out of bed, dodging as much of the rain as I could, and headed for the school tuck shop. I threw the door open and stepped into complete chaos.

'**Aargh! Look out!** A blanket, a blanket, get me a blanket! Something, anything …!'

The yelling was indeed coming from Boskin. The old caretaker had set something on fire on top of the stove and the flames were spreading quickly in spite of the rain. He was leaping around trying to beat them out with a damp tea towel, but I could see it wasn't doing much good because the tea towel was on fire as well.

Just at that moment Spencer came up behind me,

looking like a drowned rat. (Well, mouse, actually.) The rest of her gang followed her, looking equally bedraggled.

'Find a fire blanket!' I yelled over all the noise.

'You mean like this one?' she yelled back, grabbing a red package off the wall near the door. It had the words **FIRE BLANKET** printed on it in big white letters.

'That should do nicely,' I shouted. Although she probably didn't hear me.

I shook the blanket out of its packet, strode across the room and spread it out over the flames. They died down instantly and smoke began to billow across the room. I grabbed the flaming tea towel from Boskin's bony hand and pushed that under the blanket as well.

I turned to the gang. 'Someone go and work out how to turn off the school sprinkler system before we all drown.'

Garry and Larry dashed off towards the amenities block while we all stood there watching the smoke and steam rise from the stove, and the rain fall from the sprinklers over our heads. Suddenly, with a hiss and a splutter, the sprinklers switched themselves off and all was silent.

Boskin looked around at everyone, and finally his eyes settled on me.

'Bacon is off the menu for this morning,' he said.

****

'We can't be in two places at once,' said Spencer.

'I know that,' I answered. 'We just have to work out our priorities.'

We were having our usual breakfast discussion (only without the bacon). Once again, I was using my enormous police brain to work out what we should do, and the River Road Mouse Gang were listening with amazement as I unveiled the brilliance of my plan.

Or something like that.

'It'll never work, Ocko,' said Spencer. 'It'll never work.'

'What'll never work?'

'Whatever it is you're planning. If you follow the Borrow brothers and try to stop the poison attack, then Kurt and the Mayor will escape with all the town's money. And if you go off to the station to stop Kurt Remarque, then the Borrow brothers will kill all the rodents in town.'

'So what do you suggest?'

'There's only one thing for it,' said Spencer. 'We have to split up. You chase after Kurt and the Mayor, and the gang and I will take care of the Borrow brothers.'

She put down her coffee cup and stared hard at me. 'You just have to trust us on this, Ocko. Rats and mice, working together. **Don't you see that's the only way?**'

I rubbed my chin. I pulled on my whiskers. I flicked my tail a few times. I drank the last of my coffee.

And then I spoke.

'It won't work, Spencer.'

She got up from the table angrily. 'Of course it won't work, Inspector, because you just don't trust us, do you?! After all we've been through, we're still just a bunch of **dirty little mice** to you, aren't we? Dirty little criminal mice.'

'Now, wait just a minute!' I said, getting up from the table too. The rest of the gang were all watching us, but saying nothing. 'It's not about trust, Spencer, it's about common sense.'

'Sure it is,' she said, her voice full of sarcasm.

'Look, I'm serious. I **do** trust you, but don't you see? We're going up against a couple of humans who'll be carting around enough poison to kill us all. If we split up, we're taking an unacceptable risk. It's as simple as that. I know you're a great gang, and everybody knows I'm a great detective. Possibly the greatest. Ever.'

'Just get to the point, O'Malley.'

'The point, Spencer, is that we need every bit of strength we've got. We need all our numbers, all of us working together, to face this danger. And even then, we're going to need a lot of luck as well.'

'So what about the Mayor? And Kurt Remarque? And all the town's money?'

'I still think we can stop them too, but letting them escape is a risk that I'm prepared to take. Let's just save the town first, and see what happens after that. '

Spencer sighed and sat back down at the table.

'I still reckon you don't really trust us, but maybe you're right about the poison. So, out with it. What's the big Octavius O'Malley plan to foil the Borrow brothers? We know when they're going to use the poison, but we don't know where, do we? Have you forgotten that small detail? We could be chasing our tails all night and still miss them by miles.'

'No problem,' I said, with a lot more confidence than I felt. 'Remember their vehicle? The black van outside their warehouse? They're going to have to use that to carry all the poison and the hoses, so we just hide ourselves in the van overnight, hitch a ride to the spot where they're setting up their operation, then pounce.'

'**Pounce?**' asked Spencer, raising her eyebrows.

'**Pounce.**' I said proudly.

'So we just follow them, then stop them?'

'Exactly.'

'Well, that's a pretty obvious plan.'

I smiled.

'Don't worry, Spencer,' I said. 'All the best ones are.'

It was Saturday night. Midnight. I was creeping down the alleyway that led to the Borrow Brothers warehouse, trying to look casual and relaxed. Behind me, in the shadows of doorways, lurked Boskin and the River Road Mouse Gang, following me and watching for signs of trouble.

It had been raining, and the streets were a shiny black. Usually the rain made everything look soft and

clean, but tonight I couldn't help thinking that if we failed, the streets of Rodent City would soon be black and wet with poison. The thought made me shudder.

'Is this the one?' whispered Boskin. Unfortunately, Boskin's whisper was so loud and screechy that he might as well have been shouting at the top of his voice.

'For goodness' sake!' I hissed. 'Keep your voice down!'

'I'm whispering!' yelled Boskin in his best whisper.

'Anyway, this is it,' I said quickly. 'Now, quieten down or we'll have every pest controller in the street wide awake.'

Ahead of us, the dark hulking shape of the Borrow Brothers warehouse loomed up out of the darkness, and in front of it I could just make out the black van. It was covered in raindrops, which glistened in the reflection from a lone streetlight. It looked somehow

dangerous. It looked as if anyone walking by would surely guess that it was filled with menace — filled with deadly poison.

As we got closer I touched Boskin's arm, and we slowed down to give Spencer and the gang time to catch up.

'All right, Patrick the Magnificent,' I whispered, 'time to do your stuff.'

Out came the toothpick and the chewing gum, there was a bit of fiddling and then Patrick stood back proudly as the double back doors of the van popped open.

I looked cautiously inside.

Drums of poison were stacked from floor to ceiling, filling up every bit of space in the van. They were only small, each about the size of a bucket. They were bright red, and printed on the side of each was a skull and cross bones.

'There must be hundreds of them,' muttered Garry, who had moved up beside me to peek in.

'Four hundred, to be exact,' I answered. 'At least, that's what the Borrow brothers said, and looking at all this lot, I believe them.'

'So where are the hoses and all the rest of the pumping gear?' said Spencer.

'They must already be in position,' I said. 'They'll bring the poison down in the van in the morning, hook it all up, and *whoosh!* But thanks to our cunning plan, we'll be hiding in the van and ready to stop them.'

'One small problem,' mumbled Patrick the Magnificent, peering into the back of the van. 'Where do we hide in this thing? The poison is taking up every inch of space.'

'Yes, I see your point,' I said, scratching my whiskers. 'Any suggestions?'

'Why don't we empty out one of the poison barrels?' said Barry. 'We could clean it out, punch in a couple of air holes, and hide in there.'

'No way!' said Larry. 'I wouldn't be caught dead in one of those barrels!'

'Or to put it another way,' said Spencer, 'you **might** be caught dead in one of them. All it would take is a couple of drops of poison spilt on us, and we'd be goners.'

'Spencer is right,' I said. 'It's far too dangerous. Any other ideas?'

Silence.

'Come on, let's be logical,' I went on. 'The back of the van is filled with poison and the Borrow brothers will be sitting in the front. Where else is there?'

'The engine?' croaked Boskin. 'We could sit on top of the radiator. Of course, we'd have to mind the fan.'

'Bad idea,' I said. 'Much too hot and dangerous in there. Next?'

More silence, until finally Patrick spoke up.

'The glove box!'

'The glove box?' said Barry. 'Won't it be too small?'

'Only one way to find out,' I said.

We went to find out.

I left Larry as a lookout, and went around with Boskin and the rest of the gang to the front of the van. Patrick picked the lock on the passenger door and we climbed in. The glove box was unlocked, so we just opened it and looked inside.

There was a stack of papers, two broken pencils, a greasy paper bag with the remains of two stale doughnuts inside, three rusty screws, the head of a hammer, a length of plastic hose and six buttons, all of different colours and shapes. **How come no one ever keeps gloves in a glove box?'** I thought to myself.

Anyway, we cleared it all out and dumped it in a rubbish skip at the far end of the alley.

'So what do you think, Ocko?' said Spencer. 'Can we all fit in there?'

'I reckon we can,' I replied. 'Let's give it a try.'

I climbed in first, settling into one of the back corners. Boskin got into the other corner and Spencer squeezed in between us. Barry and Garry then squashed in front of us, and Patrick nestled in between them. It was tight, but it was possible. Patrick tied a length of cotton to the glove box lock and pulled it shut on us. It was cramped and unpleasant, but we were in.

Then Spencer spoke.

'What about Larry?'

'Whoops,' I said. 'I forgot about him. Maybe he'll just have to stay behind.'

'No way!' said Barry and Garry at once. 'It's all of us or none of us. Isn't that right, Spencer?'

'Afraid so, Ocko,' said Spencer. 'That's how a gang works.'

It took a bit of fiddling, but eventually we sorted it out. Boskin, Spencer and I sat across the back of the glove box; Larry, Barry and Garry arranged themselves across the front.

And Patrick? Patrick was in the ashtray.

We settled down for an uncomfortable few hours.

****

It was the sound of the engine that woke me up. I had dozed off somehow, despite feeling particularly squashed. I woke to the rumbling sound of the van's engine as it coughed and jerked into action.

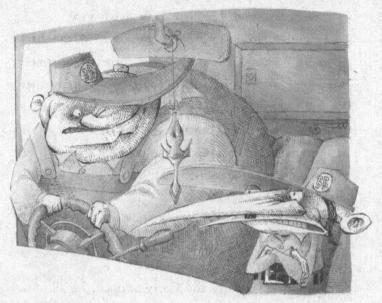

I nudged Spencer.

'We're off,' I mouthed.

Sure enough, we all felt ourselves swaying from side to side as the van pulled out from the kerb and headed down the alley. Over the sound of the engine I could just make out the occasional comment from one or the other of the Borrow brothers as they drove along.

'What time is it?'

That was the deep, rumbling grumble of Septimus, the bigger of the two brothers.

'Early,' came Gonzaga's reply. 'Just shut up and keep driving.'

'But what about breakfast? I'm starving!'

'We'll have breakfast after the job. There's no time now. Quick, take the next left.'

We all lurched inside the glove box as the van swung around a corner. The Borrow brothers picked up their conversation again, and what Septimus said next sent a chill down my spine.

'Wait! I just remembered something. I think I left a couple of doughnuts in the glove box the other day.'

'When?'

'Oh, maybe it was last week.'

'Last week? They'll be all stale by now. Forget about them.'

'Yes,' I thought to myself, 'forget about them. For heaven's sake don't open up the glove box, or we'll all be in for a nasty shock!'

'Yeah, I guess they **would** be stale by now, wouldn't they?' said Septimus wistfully.

'Stale and dry and disgusting,' said Gonzaga. 'And probably mouldy too. You should have tossed them out ages ago. Forget about them.'

I relaxed a little, and shot a nervous glance at Spencer. Maybe it would be all right.

'I **am** awfully hungry, though,' said Septimus. 'Awfully, **awfully** hungry. Maybe I could just check them out ...'

'**No!**' I thought to myself.

'**Yes,**' said Gonzaga. 'If it'll shut you up for a while, by all means check them out. Open the glove box and have a good look. Eat them, for all I care. Make yourself sick, and then I'll have to do all the work, as usual.'

Gonzaga sighed theatrically, and for a moment I hoped against hope that Septimus might take the hint and leave things alone.

I was wrong.

'Thanks. I'll just check.'

I figured we were doomed. I prepared myself for the worst, and then I heard Spencer's voice, hissing loudly from right beside me.

'Barry!' she whispered. 'Grab the latch.'

Thankfully for all of us, Barry got the idea. He was clearly smart as well as strong.

I heard a rattling sound from outside. Septimus Borrow was obviously pressing the catch, but nothing was happening. That must have been because Barry was hanging on from the inside, just like Spencer had told him to.

Septimus pressed a few more times. Barry held on.

'What on earth are you fiddling with?' asked Gonzaga.

'It's stuck,' said Septimus, continuing to press the catch.

'It can't be stuck!' said Gonzaga. 'I put a stack of papers in there just the other day.'

'Well, maybe you jammed it,' said Septimus. 'Maybe you squashed my doughnuts.'

Septimus began yanking at the lid of the glove box. Barry held on tight, but I wondered whether that huge, clumsy human would pull the lid right off the glove box and we'd all come tumbling out into Gonzaga's lap.

Septimus yanked. Barry gripped. Septimus yanked. Barry gripped. Septimus yanked. Barry gripped.

Gonzaga yelled, **'Leave it!'**

The yanking stopped.

'Just leave it alone, brother. We'll fix it later. There's no time, anyway. We're here.'

There was the low, grinding sound of a roller door from somewhere in front of us, then a bump as the van drove forward again.

I heard the roller screeching as it closed behind us, then the engine stopped.

'Whew!' I thought. 'The danger's over.'

Of course I was wrong.

'Boy, it's dark in here,' said Septimus.

'Yeah, I can't remember where the light switch is, either,' said Gonzaga. 'Get me a match so I can see what I'm doing. I think there's a matchbox in the ashtray.'

The ashtray!

17
STOP THE POISON!

We sat in the glove box, listening in the darkness —
powerless to help Patrick, or to prevent what was
about to happen.

For a few seconds, there was nothing but silence.
Septimus must have been reaching down with his fat
sausage fingers to scrabble around in the ashtray, but
we couldn't hear anything. Then suddenly we heard
something.

'AAARRGGHHH!'

It was a scream of pain, and it sounded like it had
come from Septimus Borrow.

'What is it now?' yelled Gonzaga.

'Something bit me!' said Septimus.

'Something bit you? What were you doing?'

'I was reaching into the ashtray like you said, to find
the matchbox. And something in there bit me.'

'Don't be ridiculous,' snarled Gonzaga. 'You probably
stuck one of your fat fingers into a hinge or something.
Let **me** do it.'

There was a pause, and the sound of fiddling fingers.

AAARRGGHHH!

This time the scream came from Gonzaga.

'I told you so,' said Septimus in an injured tone.

'What is it? What's going on? It's too dark to see,' said Gonzaga. 'Wait, something furry just ran up my arm!'

'We'd better get out there and help,' I said to Spencer. 'Remember, everyone, if you see a human, get stuck into him. And if you see a hose or a pipe, cut or bite through it. Whatever you can do.'

Barry thrust open the glove box and we all leapt out into complete darkness.

It was chaos. The Borrow brothers were yelling their heads off, stumbling around the room.

What is it? What ARE these things?' yelled Septimus. **'What's happening?'**

'Find the light switch **NOW!'** shouted Gonzaga.

'Get 'em, boys!' That sounded like Spencer's voice. 'Find the hoses and cut them up!'

'Who said that?' Gonzaga called out. 'How do they know about our hoses?'

As for me, your intrepid Police Inspector, I slipped out the door of the van in a calm and measured fashion, based on years of expert police training. I felt my way cautiously across the room, and for once I didn't trip over anything. Maybe I work better in complete darkness.

After a few seconds, my foot touched something cold and round. A section of hose. I yanked on it and felt it come away from whatever it was plugged into.

Then I remembered the trusty police-issue penknife in my back pocket. I pulled it out, clicked it open and began slashing through hoses wherever I could find them.

While this was happening, I could hear the Borrow brothers shouting and stumbling around, I could hear things being knocked over and rodents falling on top of each other, and I could hear barrels crashing and rolling around the room.

Barrels?

The poison! I yelled. 'Watch the poison. If those barrels break open, we're done for.'

I found another hose, bigger and wider this time, and began sawing it apart with my penknife.

I was just about through when all of a sudden I was blinded by light. One of the Borrow brothers — it was Gonzaga — had finally found the light switch on the wall.

For a second or two, we all froze, blinking, as our eyes adjusted to the light.

We were in a huge, barn-like room with a roller door. The Borrow brothers' van was parked right inside. Hoses and pipes snaked all over the floor, and as my eyes followed the tangled mess I could see that each of them was connected, one way or another, to a huge metal hydrant in the centre of the room with a giant handle on it.

Of course! It was the main pump house for the town's water supplies. It was obvious when you thought about it. By modifying the pipe system, adding a lot of extra hoses and then feeding in the contents of the barrels, the Borrow brothers could spread their deadly poison into every section of town where rats were living. (**Rats and mice**, I corrected myself.)

I took in the scene that had now been revealed. Gonzaga Borrow was standing by the wall, his hand still on the light switch and an angry, vicious scowl on his face. Patrick was hanging off his arm; he'd obviously been trying to stop him from switching on the light.

Septimus was on his back on the floor. He didn't look angry, just surprised. Larry, Barry and Garry were in a row on his stomach, pinning him in place.

I looked around for Spencer. She was off in one corner, yanking at any piece of hose she could lay her hands on, pulling it away from the twisted mess.

And Boskin? Boskin was still in the van, sitting calmly on the open lid of the glove box, looking around.

He was the first one to speak after the lights went on.

'Ah, the pump house!' he squawked in his scratchy voice. 'Of course!'

And he hopped down and scurried out.

As soon as he moved, it seemed to break the spell.

'**Rats?**' hissed Gonzaga. 'Rats … and **mice?** Is that all? Get 'em, brother!'

Gonzaga lashed out with his arm and Patrick went flying across the room and into me, knocking me backwards. Septimus rolled over and stood up, with the three mice still hanging from him. He tried to brush them off, and was able to dislodge Larry and Garry, although Barry was strong and kept holding on.

Gonzaga ran across to help his brother, but Garry climbed straight up his leg and began tickling him under one arm.

'Get off! Get off! Stupid filthy vermin!' cried Gonzaga as he wriggled and writhed.

'I hate rats,' said Septimus. 'I told you I hate rats.'

Septimus finally succeeded in knocking Barry to the ground. Spencer dashed across the room to see if he was okay.

Just then I noticed Boskin. The old caretaker had climbed right onto the handle of the hydrant that connected all the pipes and hoses.

'What are you doing?!' I yelled.

'I know this system,' explained Boskin as he fiddled with the handle. 'I know how this handle works. There was one just like it in the cheese factory, for the milk.'

As he spoke, he pushed and pulled on the handle, working it up and down, until eventually, with a grunt, he pulled it right off.

'There's one problem with the 800X-model hydrant,' he said, as he clambered down to the floor with the handle in his arms. 'If you lose the handle, there's no way to make it work. It jams up completely.'

Septimus was in one corner of the room, trying to catch up with Barry. The two of them were stumbling around three of the poison barrels that had rolled out of the back of the van in all the chaos.

But Gonzaga had heard exactly what old Boskin said, and knew he had to stop him at all costs.

'Run, Boskin, run!' I yelled. 'Get out of here, as quickly as you can, and take that handle with you!'

I looked across at the far wall, where there was a tall, narrow door.

'Head for the door!' I yelled frantically. 'Over there!'

I had noticed something interesting about that door. There was a bolt right at the top of it, but it was unlocked.

Boskin started running for his life, the heavy handle cradled in his arms. Gonzaga Borrow ran after him, and I ran after both of them.

But the old caretaker was slow, and it looked like he wasn't going to make it. He was halfway across the room. Gonzaga was closing in.

'Give me that handle, you old fool!' he shouted.

Boskin ran faster, but it wasn't fast enough. Gonzaga was just a couple of steps away now. I was close behind, but what could I do?

Suddenly something shot past me. It was Larry, the fastest mouse in the River Road Mouse Gang. Probably the fastest mouse in the universe. Who knows?

He caught up to Gonzaga, who didn't even notice him. But Gonzaga **did** notice when Larry caught hold of one of his shoelaces and pulled hard. Gonzaga Borrow went down in a tumble of arms and legs.

Boskin kept running, wheezing and panting and dragging that big handle. I climbed over Gonzaga and kept running too.

Boskin made it to the door, hauled it open and slipped through. As soon as I got to the door, I slammed it shut, then scampered up to the top of it. I grabbed the bolt at the top and slid it into place, locking the door firmly. I stayed up there, clinging to the bolt, and looked back down into the room.

Gonzaga was getting to his feet. He looked furious. He dashed up to the door, but it wouldn't open. He looked up and saw me, but the bolt was too high for him to reach.

'Septimus!' he yelled. '**Do something**, you big oaf! Help me get this door open!'

Septimus looked around the room. There was a piece of pipe lying on the floor not far away. He must have thought it might help to force the door open, because he lumbered over and grabbed it.

Spencer saw what he was doing.

'**Stop 'im, boys!**' she yelled, dashing in his direction. Garry and Barry followed, and just as Septimus picked up the pipe the three mice were on him, pulling at his arm and tangling up his legs. They all fell over backwards and crashed into the barrels of poison.

'**Careful!**' I yelled from my position on top of the door. '**Watch the poison!**'

Septimus lashed out with the piece of pipe, hoping to hit one of his attackers. He missed altogether, but the pipe whacked into the side of one of the barrels.

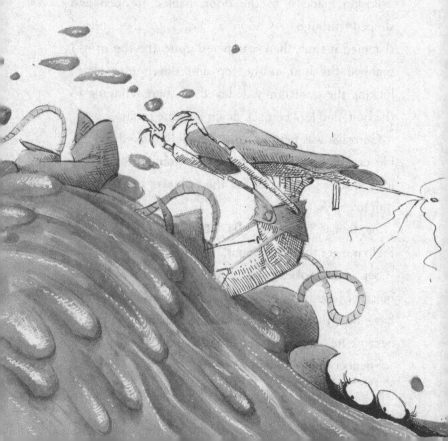

The noise was like the sound of a ship crashing into a pier. The barrel bounced across the room, crashed into one wall … and **split wide open!**

A flood of bright red poison washed across the room. I watched helplessly from above as the waves of deadly liquid picked up Spencer and Garry and Barry. The poison tide kept moving, reaching Patrick as he lay sprawled in the middle of the room, and even reaching Larry, who was still caught up in Gonzaga's shoelaces.

The Borrow brothers and I watched as the entire River Road Mouse Gang was swept along in a sea of lethal poison.

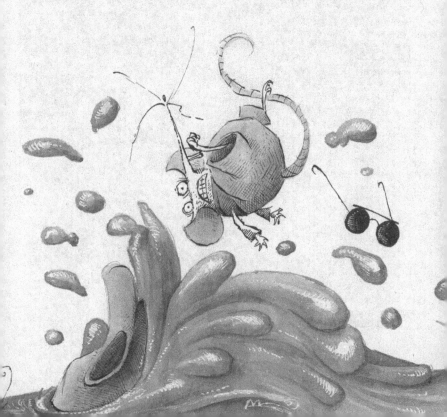

Silence. Stillness.

Five small bodies lay on the floor of the pump room, sodden lumps in a sea of red.

The Borrow brothers, poison lapping over their feet, stood like statues.

And I, Octavius O'Malley, the finest detective that ratdom has ever produced, clung helplessly to the top of a doorframe while my friends and colleagues lay sprawling below, victims of a vile and deadly poison.

I stared down at their lifeless bodies, and a sadness washed over me.

Somebody coughed.

With amazement, I saw that it was Barry. He coughed again, then with a splutter and a shudder he sat up.

How could this be? Surely his great strength was no protection against the murderous poison? Could he, alone among the River Road Mouse Gang, have survived against all the odds?

I heard another splutter. Larry sat up too. He leant over and gently prodded Garry, who groaned and started to rise as well.

Incredible!

And now Spencer herself was crawling up into a sitting position, rubbing the worst of the poison from her eyes and staring blearily around.

Her eyes fixed on Patrick, tiny Patrick.

The smallest member of the River Road Mouse Gang was still lying, unconscious, on his back.

Spencer crawled over to where Patrick the Magnificent lay and began to pump his stomach up and down with both her hands. She pumped **IN** and **OUT**, **IN** and **OUT**, five or six times, and suddenly a huge fountain of red liquid shot from Patrick's mouth and he sat bolt upright.

He stared around wildly. Then, slowly, as we all watched transfixed, his tongue poked out from between his lips and he licked, carefully and deliberately, at the lethal red poison that was still on his whiskers.

'Raspberry!' he declared.

Spencer looked at him in shock, then her own tongue popped out and tasted the red, sticky liquid that dripped from her whiskers. She smiled.

'Yes, young Patrick, I believe you may be right. Raspberry. Raspberry cordial, in fact.'

'Raspberry cordial??!!'

This came from Gonzaga Borrow.

'Raspberry cordial?? What do you mean, raspberry cordial??'

Gonzaga reached down and dipped his finger into the red puddle at his feet. Then he touched it to his lips.

'Raspberry cordial,' he hissed from between his gritted teeth.

Septimus Borrow had already begun edging uneasily towards the bolted door. His smaller brother advanced towards him, speaking in an ominously calm tone.

'Raspberry cordial, Septimus? How do you explain this little tiny problem, Septimus? I send you out for poison, Septimus. A fairly simple request, I would have thought, Septimus. I send you out for poison and you come back with **CORDIAL???**'

Septimus had backed his way right across the room to the door, but Gonzaga had followed him. I could see where this was heading, so I quickly and quietly unbolted the door.

'But ... but ... b-but they promised me it was top-quality poison. They promised!'

'They **promised?**' yelled Gonzaga. 'You did the most important business deal in our life based on a **promise?**'

Gonzaga took a step closer to his brother.

'Tell me you tested a sample of it, Septimus. Please tell me you tested a sample. Then maybe, just maybe, this is the one bad barrel. Maybe the rest will be okay.'

Septimus Borrow looked around the room in despair.

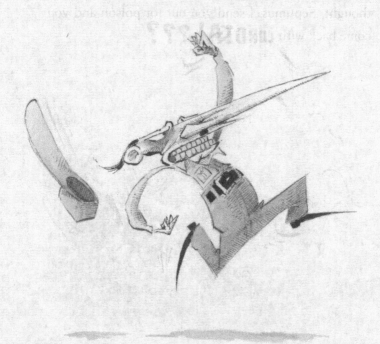

'It all came from one huge tanker,' he said. 'I watched Mr Filch fill every barrel.'

'MR FILCH!!!'

Gonzaga Borrow stepped forward and grabbed Septimus by the shirt. He had to reach up high and stand on tiptoes to do it, but somehow he managed it and began shaking his huge brother by the lapels. Septimus wobbled like a giant jelly.

'Bartholomew Filch from Filch and Fleabody??? The biggest crooks in town? The only people in the county

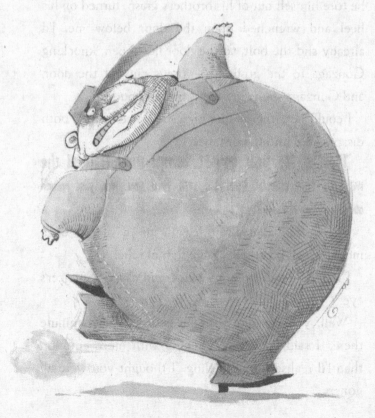

who can teach the Borrow Brothers a thing or two about lying, cheating and stealing? You bought our poison from **them?**'

'But it was such a good deal, Gonzaga. It was a great price.'

'Of course it was a great price, you huge lump of stupidity! It's **CORDIAL!!!**'

It was at this point that Septimus obviously realised he'd made every strong argument he had at his disposal, with very little success. With a huge wriggle, he tore himself out of his brother's grasp, turned on his heel and wrenched open the door below me. I'd already slid the bolt, so the door flew open, knocking Gonzaga to the ground. Septimus ran out the door, and Gonzaga staggered to his feet and pursued.

I could hear the smaller brother's voice as they both disappeared into the distance.

'**That's it, you great lump! Run! Run all the way to the county line. I'll still find you. You just ruined our one chance of a fortune ...**'

The voice faded away, leaving us in silence once more. We all breathed a huge sigh of relief.

I looked down from my perch and caught Spencer's eye.

'Well, you certainly had me worried for a minute there,' I said, my voice choking with more emotion than I'd realised I was feeling. 'I thought you were all goners.'

'Well, to be honest,' said Spencer, 'so did I. Cordial, eh? Who would've thought it?'

'Not me, that's for sure,' put in Patrick, who had completely recovered by now. 'But listen, what are we going to do about Kurt Remarque? And the Mayor?'

'Of course!' said Spencer. 'I'd forgotten all about them. They've got that bank cheque, and they'll be at the station by now. Once they realise the poison plot was a failure, they're just as likely to disappear. We'll never see them or the money again.'

'There's not a moment to lose,' I said. 'I'm off to the station.'

'What about us?' said Spencer. 'Give us a few minutes to wash all this sticky cordial off and we'll come with you.'

'There's no time,' I said, clambering down the doorframe and jumping clear of the cordial. 'As it is, I'll be lucky to make it before the train leaves.'

'But we're a **team!**' said Spencer. 'We can't split up now!'

'Don't worry,' I told them. 'I'll dash on ahead, you try and catch up. Anyway, I can handle Kurt Remarque and the Mayor.'

As I rushed out the door, I was wishing I felt as confident as I sounded.

19

THE TRAIN!

Central Station is a busy, frightening place even if you're a monkey person, but if you're a rat or a mouse it's a nightmare. On the positive side, you don't need a ticket. On the negative side, you need to make sure no one sees you. And when there are millions of passengers coming and going, trains pulling in and out all the time, and station staff manning security points to make sure no one sneaks through, it's a real challenge, even for an experienced Police Inspector like me.

Luckily, it was early Sunday morning, and no trains had left yet. That meant the crowds weren't too bad, although every bunch of humans who walked past me seemed to be carrying a picnic basket and deck chairs and huge inflatable beach balls.

I was crouched inside a rubbish bin just opposite the ticket booths. Embarrassing, I know, but I didn't have much choice. I'd been just about to creep through onto the platform about ten minutes earlier when a big crowd of teenage monkey people had come rushing through and I'd had to hastily jump for cover. It was the only spot I could find.

Now I peeked out at the station clock on the wall. 5.59am. I had six minutes to make it onto the coastal train and arrest Kurt Remarque and his cronies, or they'd be home and free. And I wasn't about to let **that** happen.

As I watched, the clock ticked over another minute, and began to chime. Six o'clock precisely.

I was just about to get really worried when I had a stroke of luck. A huge man carrying a cane picnic basket was just passing my rubbish bin as the clock struck six. He slowed down and looked up at the clock.

It was all the time I needed. While the man was distracted, I scampered up the side of the bin, flicked the catch on his picnic basket and climbed inside it. At last I was off.

I settled down in the swaying basket, making myself comfortable by leaning up against a bottle of cider as I was carried safely through the ticket barrier and towards the train.

I must admit I looked around inside just in case there were any stray doughnuts about, but there were only a few pieces of dried fruit, a loaf of bread and a big chunk of salami. I nibbled on a dried apricot as we bumped along.

A couple of minutes passed, then I felt myself being swung upwards and then plonked down on a solid piece of floor.

A minute or two later I felt a sudden jerk and a shudder as the train moved away from the platform. We were off! The basket was lifted high into the air before coming to rest once more.

I waited another minute, then slowly pushed the lid of the basket open a centimetre or two. Very quietly and cautiously I slipped out.

As I suspected, I was up in the luggage rack, conveniently away from prying eyes. But which way was it to the restaurant car, where — if my information was correct — Kurt and his cohorts were hiding themselves inside a storage bin?

I could have gone wandering aimlessly up and down the train, searching for the restaurant car and hoping no one saw me, but years of police experience had taught me to be patient in these situations, so I waited.

Sure enough, after a while the man who'd carried me onto the train reached into a pouch on the back of the seat in front of him and pulled out a menu. He ran his finger slowly down the list until it stopped next to the words *Flat white coffee — $2.50*.

He fumbled in his pocket for change, got to his feet with a grunt and swayed down the carriage and through the door at the far end.

Now I knew which way the restaurant car was; I just had to get there somehow. I certainly couldn't march boldly down the aisle and through the door. But for those of us who inhabit the rodent world, there's always another way.

Trains have electrical wiring running under the floors of the carriages, and those wires are contained in a stout metal tube for protection. Every rat worth his cheese knows that. For you humans, that tube is an invisible part of the train's structure — most of you probably don't even know it exists. But to us rats, that tube is a private corridor to anywhere we want to go.

I lowered myself out of the luggage rack, slipped down onto the man's empty seat then dropped to the floor. I could see the small service hatch that led into the tube, for when the electricians need to get in and fix a broken wire. It was halfway down the carriage, right next to a pair of women's feet.

The feet, of course, were attached to a pair of

women's legs, which were attached to a woman. This was going to be tricky.

I moved cautiously under the seats, avoiding bags and legs and dropped pieces of rubbish, until I came to where the woman was sitting.

Now that I was closer, I could see that it was even worse than I'd thought. Her right foot was directly on top of the service hatch.

I had two choices: I could wait until she changed position, or I could take more direct action.

I'm not proud of what I did. I took no pleasure in it. But sometimes a rat's got to do what a rat's got to do.

I bit her ankle.

The woman looked down to see what the strange pricking sensation was. I waved at her and smiled.

'EEEK! A MOUSE! A MOUSE ON THE TRAIN!'

She lifted both feet into the air and scrambled up onto the seat. That was exactly what I needed. While she yelled and screamed and all the other passengers looked around to see what was happening, I slipped open the hatch and dived in.

All the while, I was thinking to myself, '**A mouse?** She thought I was **a mouse?** What's the world coming to?'

Anyway, I was on my way. The tube was a tight fit, but I squeezed along it in the direction the man had taken. After several metres, I came to a soft, rubbery section, which was obviously the connecting part between two carriages.

I kept going, through three more carriages. Each time the tube entered a new carriage there was a smaller tube running off it, feeding electricity to the carriage itself.

As I entered a fourth carriage, I noticed that the smaller tube running off was larger, and there were lots and lots of wires.

Why would one carriage need lots more electricity than any of the others? Well, think of electric hotplates and jugs and dishwashers. Think of refrigerators and electric cash registers. That's right, I was in the dining car.

I wriggled through into the smaller tube, wishing I hadn't eaten so many doughnuts over the past few years.

After several minutes of squirming and sweating and sucking in my rather-too-fat stomach, I had reached the end of the tube, and I popped out to find myself — behind the refrigerator.

Perfect! Out of sight and safe.

Now I had to find the storage bin. I peeked around the side of the fridge. On the opposite wall of the carriage was a small door marked **STORAGE BINS**. How easy was this?

I made a dash for it, scooting across the floor. I heard no shrieks or screams, so I guess nobody saw me. I pushed open the door marked **STORAGE BINS** and slipped in.

I was in a sort of walk-in pantry. There were shelves right up to the ceiling, stacked with all sorts of tins and packets.

There were also three big storage bins. One was marked **POTATOES**. One was marked **ONIONS**. The third was marked **DEEP-FRIED LITHUANIAN ASPARAGUS STRANDS**.

I opened the first bin. Potatoes. I opened the second bin. Onions. I opened the third bin, and fell in.

20
INSIDE THE BIN

I should've known there was no
such thing as deep-fried Lithuanian
asparagus strands. Or if there were,
who on earth would order them on
a train?

I was tumbling down a long
chute. It was pitch black, so there
was nothing to see as I fell head
over tail downwards.

Then I hit the
bottom, and there
was plenty to see.

I had landed in what looked like a dining room. A beautifully furnished, luxurious, rat-sized dining room. There was a table set for breakfast, with plates, cutlery and cups laid out for seven. There were comfy chairs set back against the walls and a couch with a reading lamp in one corner. Next to the reading lamp was a small side table, and on it was a small piece of paper. I strode across the room and picked it up.

It was a cheque drawn on the Rodent City Public Bank. It was for $523,765, and it was made out to 'CASH'. The account the money came from was written across the top: RODENT CITY COMMUNITY ASSET ACCOUNT.

Could it be this easy? I had the stolen cheque right here in my hands, and all I had to do was tear it up, then arrest everyone. (Once I found them, of course.)

'O'Malley,' I said to myself, 'some days you just get lucky.'

'Ahem.'

It was the sound of someone clearing their throat. I turned around and found myself staring straight into the pale pink eyes of Kurt Remarque.

'I think you have something there that belongs to me,' he said.

Even as he spoke, the door behind him opened wider and a group of other rats walked into the room. I saw Mayor Mottley, Police Chief Carey, Deputy Police Chief Jenkins and the other three main plotters

— Crumbley the baker, Patterson the jeweller and Vellum the electricity company manager.

'What's going on, O'Malley?' barked the Police Chief, coming to stand beside Kurt Remarque.

The breakfast table was between us. I wondered how long it would take them to get around it and grab me. I looked about for an escape route; there wasn't one.

The only door I could see was the one the plotters had
come out of, and there was no way I could push myself
back up the dark chute I'd come down.

'I said, "What's going on, O'Malley?" I thought you
were deep undercover, chasing the River Road Mouse
Gang. What are you doing on this train, with Kurt
Remarque's … um … property in your hand?'

'You know exactly what I'm doing, sir,' I replied. 'I'm doing my job. In fact, I'm investigating the biggest case of my career.'

'I don't know what you're talking about,' said the Police Chief.

'Look, enough of this,' Kurt Remarque interrupted. 'O'Malley, you're a fool. Put the cheque down. Don't you know when you're outclassed?'

He took a step forward and leant both of his massive arms on the breakfast table. He never once took those cold, pale eyes off mine.

'You'd better work out what side you're on, O'Malley,' he went on. 'You think you're going to arrest us and take us back to Rodent City? Fool! There **is** no Rodent City. The Rodent City you know has gone, and in its place I will build a new one. A better one. You can be part of that too ...'

'The poison didn't work.'

With those four words, I stopped Kurt Remarque in mid-speech. He stared hard at me and said nothing for several seconds. Then his eyes narrowed.

'What did you say?' he hissed.

'You heard me, Kurt. The poison didn't work. In fact, there **was** no poison. Those idiots you threw in your lot with couldn't even get that right. Right now, the Rodent City pump house is awash with red cordial. It's a mess, but I expect it'll get cleaned up sooner or later. Just like I'm cleaning up you lot now. **You're all under arrest**.'

'It wasn't my fault!' protested Mayor Mottley, stepping away from the others. 'I had no choice. Kurt Remarque made me do it. I'm sick. I didn't know what I was doing. I had no idea.'

'That's more than enough excuses, Mayor,' I said, 'and I don't believe any of them. You were greedy, that's what it was.' I looked around the room. 'You were **all** greedy. You didn't care about your fellow rats, you didn't care about the community you lived in, and you certainly didn't care about the mice who would die as well. All you cared about was money.'

I turned to look at Police Chief Carey and his Deputy, Jenkins. 'What I really don't understand is you, sir. And you, Deputy Jenkins. You both swore to uphold the law. How could you let yourselves get involved in this evil plot?'

Police Chief Carey looked as though he wished the floor would open up and swallow him. He gazed at me with a sigh, and his shoulders dropped.

'O'Malley, what can I tell you? It seemed like a good idea at the time. You know the humans will always keep trying to poison us, to destroy us, to drive us away. Sooner or later they'll succeed. This at least seemed like a way to get something good out of the inevitable.'

'Enough!' Kurt Remarque had obviously run out of patience. Then again, maybe he never had any patience to begin with. Maybe he was just standing there thinking about all that red cordial.

'Gentlemen,' he said, 'it's time to cut our losses. We'll take what we can out of this sorry mess. And that means ...' Kurt Remarque began to move slowly around the table towards me. 'That means, Inspector, that I'm afraid I'm going to need that cheque, if you would be so kind.'

I stood there watching as Kurt Remarque and the other plotters began to close in on me. I had my back to the wall. The original cornered rat. There was no one to help me.

What would **you** have done? Imagine yourself in my position, and then try to imagine you are a world-famous police detective with years of training and experience. What would **you** do?

Well, I knew immediately what to do.

I ate the cheque.

It tasted terrible, but I didn't spend too long savouring it. I stuffed it into my mouth as Kurt Remarque came rushing round the table. I quickly chewed it as he knocked me to the ground, and then I swallowed it completely as Crumbley and Patterson sat on me.

Then I looked up into Kurt Remarque's furious face.

'Anything to drink?' I asked innocently.

****

Half an hour later I was sitting in one of the comfy chairs, tied up securely, while Kurt and his fellow plotters discussed their next move.

'I say we kill him,' said Kurt.

'I've told you once, and I'll tell you again,' said Police Chief Carey. 'We're not killing one of my officers.'

'Look,' said Kurt, 'we need to buy ourselves time. And we can't do that with this meddlesome rat in our way.'

'What good does it do to buy ourselves time?' asked the Mayor. 'The whole thing's a disaster. The attack failed, we've lost the ten million dollars, and we're all going to go to gaol.'

'That's typical of you, Mottley. You're a waste of space.'

'You got us all into this, Kurt,' said the Mayor petulantly. 'I wish I'd never listened to you.'

'Just calm down,' said Kurt, 'and listen. We get rid of O'Malley. That buys us time. We're stuck on this train for now, but as soon as it reaches the coast, we take the next train back to Rodent City. Mottley, you write a new cheque for the city's money. I'll draw my own funds out of all my accounts. And then we're out of here, to start a new life somewhere else.'

'But that's impossible,' said the Mayor. 'Isn't it?'

'Mottley, nothing is impossible unless and until I say it is!' snapped Kurt Remarque. 'Get with the program. We're getting out of Rodent City and taking everything we can with us. That's why we need some time to get organised, and that's why we need to get rid of O'Malley.'

'Look, I agree,' said Police Chief Carey, 'but we're not going to kill him. There has to be another way. We just need a few hours.'

'I've got an idea,' said Patterson the jeweller. 'Your safe.'

'What about my safe?' asked Kurt.

'Stick the Police Inspector in there. Drop him off the train. Someone will find him by the side of the track eventually and let him out, but by then we'll be long gone.'

'What if they **don't** find him?' said Deputy Jenkins. 'What if he suffocates in there?'

'Oh, I think that's … unlikely,' said Kurt Remarque, rubbing his whiskers slowly. 'Yes, Patterson, your plan might just work. Anyone got any better ideas?'

'Yeah, just let him go and give yourselves up!'

'Nice try, O'Malley. You just keep quiet,' ordered Kurt.

Patterson and Crumbley went out through the door they'd all come in by. It must lead to a bedroom or something. Not a bad set-up, this so-called 'storage bin'.

Anyway, they came straight back, wheeling a big steel safe between them, straining under the weight. They put it down on the floor with a *THUMP*.

Kurt Remarque knelt down in front of it and began to fiddle with the big combination lock on the front.

'Are you sure this is a smart idea?' said Police Chief Carey.

'It's the **only** idea,' replied Kurt, as the safe door swung open and he began to empty things out of it. I saw a few documents, and a lot of cash.

'Sorry, Ocko,' said the Police Chief. 'Next time I suggest you mind your own business.'

'I didn't get to be the best police detective in town by minding my own business, sir,' I said, 'so I don't think I should start now.'

Kurt Remarque walked over to one corner of the room, pulled back the carpet and swung open a trapdoor. I could hear the **CLICKETY-CLACK** of the wheels on the rails.

Patterson and Crumbley took me by the arms and bundled me into the safe.

'You'll be sorry!' I yelled as they slammed the safe door on me. 'Yeah, good one, Ocko,' I thought to myself. 'That's telling them.'

I heard the combination dial being turned. I felt myself moving as they pushed the safe across the floor towards the open trapdoor. The noise of the train became louder and louder, and suddenly I was tumbling, falling through space. There was a huge **BUMP** as I hit the ground, then the safe began rolling down the embankment.

At some point I must have hit my head on the side of the safe and passed out. The last thing I remember thinking was: 'How much air is in this thing?'

When I came to it was dark and hot and airless. I had no idea what time it was, or how long I'd been inside the safe. I rubbed the side of my head, which was still a little sore from the bump, and tried to think straight. What now?

I felt around inside the safe. It was completely empty, apart from having a rather annoyed and slightly worried Police Inspector inside it.

I felt around the walls of the safe until I found the door. There was a bump in the middle of it that must be the combination lock, but there seemed to be no way to open it from the inside. I guess safe manufacturers never think about someone being locked inside them. Why would they? After all, who expects there to be dirty rats in the world like Kurt Remarque, rats who would help poison their own community if they thought it would make them a profit ...

Then I heard scratching. Somewhere outside the safe. No, not scratching, more like clicking, or, or ...

turning. It was the combination dial! Somebody was turning the combination dial!

I started thumping on the walls of the safe, but soon gave up. The walls were so thick that I was sure no one outside would hear a thing, and besides, the air was so stale and stuffy that I soon wore myself out. I sat back down on the floor of the safe, panting a little, and listened to the slow, deliberate turning of the lock.

Were they trying to open it? And if they were, what were the chances that they'd be able to work out the combination? All in all, my prospects of being saved were not great, but at least someone had stumbled across the safe. That was a start.

The noise stopped. Why had it stopped? Had they given up? Were they going away?

Suddenly the door of the safe swung open and a wave of sunlight burst in, blinding me temporarily. I rubbed my eyes with both hands and stumbled forward into the outside world. I took a deep breath of beautiful, clean, fresh air and opened my eyes ... to find myself staring at a familiar face.

'**Boskin!** Boskin, you **genius!** How did you ...? Where did you ...? What did you ...?'

'Calm down!' screeched Boskin in his scratchy, hoarse voice. I'd never been so happy to hear it. 'You're not making any sense.'

'Oh, Boskin, you're a **legend!** How did you find me? And how did you get this safe open?'

'First things first,' said the old caretaker. 'Have a drink of this. I brought it with me from the train.'

I took the water bottle from his bony hand and swallowed a huge mouthful, and then I realised what he'd said.

'You were on the train?'

'Too right I was on the train,' he said. 'I knew that was where Kurt Remarque would be, and I figured you lot would be heading in that direction too. As soon as I'd hidden the pump handle, that was where I went.'

'But I was on the train too,' I said. 'Why didn't I see you?'

'I went into the wrong bin,' rasped Boskin. 'It was the onion bin instead of the deep-fried Lithuanian asparagus strands bin.'

'I didn't see you when I looked in the onion bin.'

'Yes, well, I was hiding,' explained Boskin. 'I wasn't sure who you were at first.'

'So why didn't you follow me into the **right** bin, into the storage locker?'

'Well, I did,' responded Boskin. 'Eventually.'

'Eventually?'

'Well, you know how much I like onions. And I hadn't eaten a thing for ages. A rat my age needs to keep his strength up, you know. So I peeled a couple of onions and ate them. Just to take the edge off my hunger, you know. And then ...'

'And then?'

'Well, then I had a little nap.'

'You had **a little nap?** I shouted. '**A little nap?** I'm there battling the bad guys, and you're **napping?**'

'Well, I didn't mean to,' added Boskin quickly, 'it just happened. One minute I was taking another layer off an onion and nibbling away, the next I was snoring like a baby. I don't know how long I slept, but I woke up to hear a loud clunking and banging noise coming from the storage bin next to me. I opened the lid and heard Kurt Remarque say something about dumping that troublesome O'Malley, and it didn't take a mastermind to work out the rest.'

'So you came after me?' I said gratefully.

'You bet!' rasped Boskin proudly. 'Off the train I went, down the embankment, and I soon found you.'

'And the combination?'

'I know all KR's combinations,' he answered. 'Old Boskin is no fool.'

He took back his water bottle and had a sip himself, while I dusted off my trousers and got to my feet.

'What now, Inspector?' he said.

'Now we hurry,' I said, looking around at the scenery. 'Two questions, Boskin. First: do you have any idea where the nearest road back to Rodent City is?'

'How would I know?' grumbled Boskin 'What do you think I am — a street directory?'

'Well, luckily, I **do** know,' I said. 'It's about half a kilometre that way. I pointed over his shoulder. 'It's the main highway, and it goes straight into the centre of town. Now, follow me. We don't have a moment to lose.'

'What was the second question?' asked Boskin as he fell in beside me.

'The second question?' I replied. 'Oh yes, the second question. Do you know the best way of hijacking a monkey person's car and getting a free ride back to town?'

'No idea,' said Boskin.

'Then watch and learn,' I said. 'Watch and learn.'

****

Twenty minutes later Boskin and I were crouched patiently behind a wild rose bush at the side of the main highway, waiting for a car. Stretched across the

road in front of us was a long, thin branch from the bush, its thorns pointing dangerously into the air.

'Are you sure this will work?' asked Boskin, looking at me as if I were an idiot.

'Of course,' I answered confidently, 'I've thought this all through very carefully. Those thorns are razor-sharp. The car drives over them, gets a flat tyre and has to stop. While the humans change the tyre, we sneak into the car and we're on our way.'

'But car tyres are solid as a rock,' objected Boskin. 'Have you ever tried to cut one? Or puncture one? Those thorns will never break through.'

'Of course they will,' I said.

'Okay, let's say they do,' went on Boskin. 'Although I still say they won't. But if they do, why won't they puncture two of the car's tyres? Or three, or even all four? How many spare tyres does one car carry?'

'Shut up,' I interrupted, 'someone's coming.'

A big family car came over the hill towards us. We shrank down behind the bush as it hurtled past — its tyres grinding the thorny branch into the ground as it went right over the top of it.

'See?' squawked Boskin. 'I **told** you it was a stupid idea. This will never work.'

'Got any better suggestions?' I said irritably. 'At least I'm making an effort.'

As we continued with this entertaining and very constructive conversation, a second vehicle came over the hill. It was an open-backed truck loaded with boxes. Unbelievably, it began to slow down as it approached us.

Boskin and I crouched right down behind the bush as the truck came to a complete stop right next to us.

A man in dirty overalls climbed down from the cabin, followed by a small girl.

'Right,' he said, 'you've got two minutes, then we'll have to get a move on. I need to get these tomatoes to the city market as soon as I can.'

'I want four roses,' said the little girl. 'Mummy will love them! Will you pick them for me, Daddy? The thorns are too sharp.'

The man took the little girl's hand, and they both headed right for the bush we were hiding behind.

Boskin and I waited until they were leaning over, concentrating on picking the best of the bright red roses on the bush, then we slipped out and scuttled up the back of the truck.

Let me give you a piece of advice. If you're planning a long road trip, there's nothing more comfortable than a bed of slightly ripe, fragrant tomatoes. Boskin and I settled back on the tomatoes, hands behind our heads, and looked up at the bright blue sky and the scudding clouds as we rumbled closer to town.

'Sometimes you just get lucky,' I said with a smile, reaching for a tomato and taking a warm, juicy mouthful.

22
PAYBACK TIME

I strode into the main room of the old schoolhouse with Boskin right behind me.

The River Road Mouse Gang were sitting round the table with steaming mugs of coffee in their hands. They all looked up at the same time and Spencer jumped to her feet in alarm.

'Ocko!' she cried, rushing over to me. 'Where have you been?'

As she got closer to me, she looked even more worried. 'What's wrong with your face? Is that ... is that **blood?** Are you **hurt?**'

I reached up and wiped my face, then looked at my hand.

'No, it's tomato,' I replied nonchalantly.

'Tomato?'

'Never mind about that,' I said. 'I've come from the train. Boskin helped me.'

'We headed for the station as soon as we cleaned all that cordial off,' put in Patrick, 'but we were too late.

The train had already gone. So we came back here to wait.'

I sat down and told them all about what had happened on the train.

'... so I figure we've got a couple of hours at best before they're all back in town. They're going to try and take all the city's money and hotfoot it out of here. Any suggestions about how to stop them?'

'Arrest them,' said Patrick. 'Lock them up.'

'I thought of that,' I told them, 'but I'm not sure it would work. I've already tried it once, and it didn't get me too far.'

'But this time, you get reinforcements,' went on Patrick. 'Get a few other policerats, ones that you trust, and round up every one of those crooks. After all, those minutes are all the proof you need to put them behind bars for years.'

'Hmm, I'm not so sure,' I mused. 'The minutes **might** work, but Kurt could always deny it all. And if the Police Chief and the Mayor and everyone else deny it, who do you think the judge would believe?'

'Even with the minutes as proof?' said Patrick.

'Even with the minutes,' I said. 'Who's to say Kurt Remarque and his assistant weren't just writing a novel, loosely based on reality? The only real proof would be the Borrow brothers, but I don't think we'll be seeing **them** again.'

'Yeah, you're right,' said Patrick. 'And after all, what has anyone really done that looks so bad on paper? So someone spilt a bit of red cordial.'

They all sipped their coffee, and I rubbed my chin.

'Well,' I said slowly, 'if no one can think of anything else, then I guess arresting them is the only thing I can try. I suppose I could get Sergeant Smith, and a couple of constables —'

'Wait!' said Spencer. 'I've got an idea.'

She put her cup down and turned to Patrick.

'Pat,' she said, her eyes lit up with excitement, 'do you remember that time we held up the First Rodent Bank?'

'Sure do,' said Patrick.

'I'm going to pretend I didn't hear that,' I said in my best official police voice.

'And do you remember what you said then about computers?' went on Spencer, after glancing cautiously in my direction.

'Yes,' said Patrick slowly. 'I said if you break into a computer instead of a bank branch, you don't need guns or masks, and you can do a whole lot more.'

'Exactly!' said Spencer. 'Now, listen, Patrick the Magnificent. You can break into anything, can't you?'

'Absolutely!' said Patrick. 'Nothing can keep me out.'

'Exactly!' said Spencer again. She turned to Boskin. 'And Boskin, Ocko says you know Kurt Remarque's office pretty well.'

'You bet,' said the old caretaker. 'He trusts me with everything. I guess he thinks I'm too old and stupid to worry about.'

'So would you know things like, for example, the password for his computer? The one on his desk?'

'Off by heart,' said Boskin proudly.

'Okay,' said Spencer. 'Patrick and Boskin, come with me. We've got a lot to do, and not much time.'

'What are you going to do?' I asked, feeling more than a little worried. 'You're not going to break the law, are you?'

Spencer walked over to where I was sitting and looked at me carefully.

'Ocko, it's best you don't know. You'll just have to trust me on this one, okay? We've been through a lot together, and we both know what's right and what's wrong. Just trust me.'

I looked at this strange little mouse, whose gang I had been hunting for so long. Just a few weeks ago, I would have given anything to see her in gaol. Now I just smiled.

'I trust you,' I said.

****

The central branch of the First Rodent Bank is a beautiful building. It has high ceilings and chandeliers and lots of potted palms dotted around the room. Which was just as well, really, because I was standing discreetly behind one of those palms when Kurt

Remarque and the Mayor walked up to one of the bank tellers behind the counter.

I had my collar turned up high and my hat pushed down low, and I was standing with my back to the counter pretending to read an interesting booklet about home loans. But I was listening carefully with both of my slightly large ears. I didn't want to miss this moment for anything.

Mayor Mottley went to the counter first, a slip of paper in his hand.

The teller looked up.

'Ah, Mr Mayor, how can I help you today?'

'Um, well, there's a small problem. You see, I withdrew a **substantial** sum of money from the city accounts recently, but the cheque was ... um, **destroyed**.'

'Destroyed, sir?' asked the teller, lifting his eyebrows in surprise and twitching his whiskers.

'Yes,' the Mayor went on. 'Unaccountably lost. So I would like to withdraw everything in the account, only this time in cash.'

'Whatever you say, Mr Mayor. One moment, please.'

The teller pressed a few buttons on his computer keyboard, typed in a long string of numbers, and looked at the screen. Then he looked at the Mayor. Then he looked back at the screen.

'Um, I'm sorry, Mr Mayor, but there seems to be some sort of mix-up.'

'Mix-up?' said Mottley, his eyes darting from side to

side. I looked studiously at my booklet and hoped he hadn't seen me.

'Yes,' continued the teller smoothly. 'You see, the city account actually has no funds in it at all. It has a zero balance.'

'A zero balance? **A zero balance???**'

The teller punched a few more buttons on his computer and a sheet of paper came off the printer behind him. He picked it up, checked it quickly, then handed it across to Mottley.

'See, Mr Mayor? **Available funds: zero.** Can I help you with anything else?'

Mottley stumbled away from the counter, still clutching the sheet of paper and his own, now useless, withdrawal slip. He made his way over to Kurt Remarque.

The two rats stood there toe to toe, whispering furiously at each other and waving their arms about. I was too far away to hear most of it, but at one point Kurt Remarque raised his voice and hissed, 'Mottley, you're a hopeless fool.'

And now Kurt Remarque was stalking across the room to the same teller. He trained his beady pink eyes on the rat behind the counter and thrust a piece of paper in front of the teller's eyes. Now I could hear everything clearly again.

'Check my account, you fool, and if you tell me there's a zero balance I'll have your guts for garters.'

The teller gulped nervously, and once more began punching numbers into his computer. He scanned the screen for a few seconds, then a smile of relief crossed his face.

'No, sir, there is no zero balance. Your account is in credit, Mr Remarque.'

Kurt Remarque grinned smugly, and ran one of his pink hands through the sleek, white fur on his head.

'Thank goodness **someone** knows what they're doing,'

he grunted. 'Now, I want to withdraw it all, do you understand? Every last penny.'

'Of course, Mr Remarque. Right away. How would you like that?'

Kurt allowed a self-satisfied smirk to cross his face. 'In two large sacks,' he said. 'Hundred-dollar notes only.'

The teller froze.

'Excuse me?'

'Hundred-dollar notes!' barked Kurt Remarque. 'Bundles and bundles of hundreds. Two large sacks. Now, get on with it!'

'But Mr Remarque,' said the teller, 'I ... you ... that is ...'

'What?' said Kurt Remarque in a voice cold enough to freeze a hot pie.

'Your account, sir,' stumbled the teller.

'What about my account?'

'Well, the balance.'

'Yes?' Kurt Remarque's voice was getting louder by the instant.

'The balance of your account is six dollars and forty-three cents.'

'What on earth are you talking about?' hissed Kurt Remarque. 'I've got **millions** in there! **Millions**, do you hear me?'

The teller looked at his screen.

'You **did** have, sir, you **did** have. But you must have forgotten. Earlier today you transferred almost everything out of the account. It was a computer transaction, according to the records I have here.'

Kurt Remarque stood there like a statue, glaring at the teller as if he could melt him with his eyes. In a voice barely above a whisper, he asked 'Who to?'

The teller began to tremble. 'Who to, sir?' he asked. 'Well, according to the information I have here, the payment was made to **River Road Enterprises**.'

I have never seen a teller move so fast.

As Kurt Remarque lunged across the counter and tried to grab the poor rat, the teller shot backwards as if he'd been pulled from behind by a rope. Then he was off.

Kurt Remarque began bellowing like a bull. Mottley went bright red under his fur.

I had seen enough. I turned and quietly left the bank.

23
POLICE CHIEF O'MALLEY

Six months have now passed since the scene in the bank, and a lot has happened in that time.

If you've read the title of this chapter carefully, you'll have noticed that I've been promoted. Which is only fair, considering what a wonderfully talented and brilliant policerat I am.

Police Chief O'Malley. Police Chief Octavius O'Malley of the Rodent City Metropolitan Police Force. Has a nice ring to it, don't you think?

Amazingly, both Police Chief Carey and his Deputy resigned at the same time a few months ago. Disappeared quietly into retirement and recommended me for promotion. Very gratifying. I now sit at my desk in this nice new office, and in my locked bottom drawer is a very interesting book. I take it out and read it every now and then when I have a quiet moment.

Unfortunately, I don't have too many quiet moments. Things are pretty busy these days. Just this morning I had Deputy Police Chief Smith in my

office, updating me on the investigations into the notorious River Road Mouse Gang.

'Nothing to report, I'm afraid, sir,' he said sadly. 'It's incredible that ever since their audacious computer theft from Mr Remarque and the City Council, they've gone completely quiet. It's almost as if they've disappeared into thin air.'

'Yes, indeed,' I told him. 'Still, keep up the inquiries, Smith. You never know what might turn up.'

He's a good rat, that Smith. Not the most brilliant police investigator in the world, but very thorough and very honest. He's keeping the traffic flowing nicely, the streets are clean, and littering is at an all-time low.

Of course, Kurt Remarque is furious that his case was never solved. We never worked out who bombed his cheese factory, and we never worked out who stole all his money from the bank.

I've heard he runs a little food stall in a rough part of town now, and all of his staff have left to work for someone else. Bit short of money these days, the old Kurt Remarque. Pity, really.

He often storms into Deputy Smith's office and demands to know how the investigation is going. Funny thing is, he never asks me. Hasn't spoken to me once since our little train trip together.

Oh yes, and Mayor Mottley resigned as well. No one blamed him for the missing city money, of course: that was the work of the notorious River Road Mouse Gang. Whoever they may be.

No, Mayor Mottley resigned over another matter all together. Apparently it took him six weeks to get the water supplies reconnected to Rodent City after the vandalism in the main pump house. Some fool spilt red cordial everywhere, then stole the pump handle. They couldn't find it for weeks. The whole town was forced to cart buckets of water back and forth, and everyone got more and more annoyed.

Even more annoying, the water was reconnected easily when an old caretaker named Boskin showed the Mayor how it was done. He designed a new handle, connected it himself, and set things to right in about five minutes.

It wasn't long before the average rat in the street was asking why Boskin wasn't the Mayor, since he seemed to be the only one who knew how to fix things. The election is next week, and I think Boskin is looking pretty good. I see him strolling up and down the streets in a fine new suit, handing out onions to passers-by and promising that when he's elected he'll keep the town spick-and-span.

Anyway, there's probably a lot more I could tell you, but I'm a bit short of time at the moment. I'm off to an important meeting this afternoon.

You see, I'm the Honorary Chair-rat of a new foundation that's been established in Rodent City. There' another meeting today, so I have to dash. It's called the **Society for the Cooperation of Rats And Mice**. We're already calling it **S.C.R.A.M.** for short. The aim of S.C.R.A.M. is to help rats and mice to understand and appreciate each other, and work together to make Rodent City the best place for rats and mice to live in the whole world.

That's a pretty ambitious idea, I know, but the society has plenty of money to work with. Some anonymous donors have provided it with millions and

millions of dollars. The first thing the society did was hand over a cheque to the City Council for $523,765, which was exactly the amount of money stolen by that nasty River Road Mouse Gang.

Today's meeting is to decide what good deeds the society should do next. One idea is to establish an annual Mouse and Rat Picnic, and invite everyone in Rodent City. We're also planning a research library, where books will be written about all the things rats and mice have in common.

Spencer will be at the meeting today. You may have heard of her — she's a very talented and intelligent mouse, and she is the Director of the Society. She's also become a good friend of mine. Fancy that, a rat who has a mouse for a friend! Still, things are changing around here. Like I said: a lot has happened in six months.

Just yesterday, I was sharing tea and doughnuts with Spencer in my office.

As I handed her the doughnut plate, she smiled and said, 'Thanks' as she helped herself to a doughnut.

'Spencer,' I said, 'do you think all rats and mice will learn to get along one day?'

'Bound to happen, Ocko, bound to happen,' she replied. 'Once this society gets to work, you'll be amazed at how quickly things will improve. The truth is, the more we find out about each other, the better it will be.'

I put down my doughnut and rubbed my whiskers.

'I guess you're right, Spencer,' I said. 'But one thing worries me.'

'Monkey people?' she asked.

'You're reading my mind,' I replied. 'You and I both know the real story, don't we? We may have outsmarted Kurt Remarque, and we may be bringing mice and rats closer together, but what about those humans?'

'What about them?' said Spencer,

'Well, they didn't manage to get rid of us this time, but you know they'll keep trying. They hate us. They want to see us dead. What are we going to do about that? What **can** we do?'

Spencer took a big bite of her doughnut, leant back in her chair, and put her tiny feet up on my desk.

'One thing at a time, Ocko,' she said. 'One thing at a time.'

THE END

Alan Sunderland is the author of three previous books, and when he's not writing he is in charge of network and state news coverage on ABC radio and television. He has worked as a journalist for twenty-seven years and won several awards, including two Walkleys. Alan lives with his wife and three sons on River Road in Sydney — which is, curiously, also the name of a notorious mouse gang.

LOOK OUT FOR ...

OCTAVIUS O'MALLEY

AND THE MYSTERY OF THE

MISSING MOUSE

**OCTAVIUS O'MALLEY, THE GREATEST RAT DETECTIVE
OF ALL, IS BACK ON THE CASE AGAIN —
ONLY THIS TIME IT'S PERSONAL!**

When his mouse friend Patrick the Magnificent goes
missing, OcKo joins in the hunt, and it doesn't take
long before the trail leads to the most evil rat ever
to stalk the streets of Rodent City: Kurt Remarque.

But finding the missing mouse is just the start of
this mystery. Before it ends, there will be helicopter
rides, buried treasure, a plot with more twists and
turns than a corkscrew, and an ending that will Keep
you on the edge of your seat!

Spencer, José and Patrick all started screaming at the same time, as we plummeted towards the ground. I tried to pull back hard on the controls to lift the front of the helicopter. For a moment, nothing happened, then we came out of our dive, straightened up … and started heading straight for the cliff face.

That was when I started screaming too.

I swerved wildly to the left and felt a loud CRUNCH as the back of the helicopter slammed against the wall. It felt as if something had fallen off. I swung back to the right and this time it was the nose of the helicopter that hit the wall. A big crack shivered across the windscreen, one of the doors fell off, and the engine stalled completely. 'This can't be good,' I thought to myself, as we plummeted once more towards the ground …